It starts with just a little hope...

"It was good seeing you."

"You, too."

But when Lillian moved off in the direction of her car, Denny couldn't help but call after her. "Should we get together tonight?"

She halted and looked in his direction, her eyes widening slightly.

"I mean to narrow down the colors—with your aunt, too, of course."

"Daylight would be better for that, don't you think?"

"Noontime tomorrow, then? I can pick up sub sandwiches and we can make it a working lunch out in the garden."

She hesitated for the briefest moment, then nodded. "Okay, sure. I'll see you then."

For whatever reason, Denny whistled a merry tune all the way to his car.

For the first time in recent memory, he was not in that much of a hurry at the moment to get himself out of Hunter Ridge...

Glynna Kaye treasures memories of growing up in small Midwestern towns—and vacations spent with the Texan side of the family. She traces her love of storytelling to the times a houseful of great-aunts and great-uncles gathered with her grandma to share candid, heartwarming, poignant and often humorous tales of their youth and young adulthood. Glynna now lives in Arizona, where she enjoys gardening, photography and the great outdoors.

Books by Glynna Kaye

Love Inspired

Hearts of Hunter Ridge

Rekindling the Widower's Heart
Claiming the Single Mom's Heart
The Pastor's Christmas Courtship
The Nanny Bargain
Mountain Country Cowboy
Mountain Country Courtship

Dreaming of Home
Second Chance Courtship
At Home in His Heart
High Country Hearts
A Canyon Springs Courtship
Pine Country Cowboy
High Country Holiday

Visit the Author Profile page at Harlequin.com for more titles.

Mountain Country Courtship

Glynna Kaye

HARLEQUIN® LOVE INSPIRED®

Recycling programs
for this product may
not exist in your area.

LOVE INSPIRED BOOKS

ISBN-13: 978-1-335-50944-4

Mountain Country Courtship

Copyright © 2018 by Glynna Kaye Sirpless

www.Harlequin.com

Printed in U.S.A.

Herein is love, not that we loved God,
but that he loved us, and sent his Son
to be the propitiation for our sins.
—*1 John* 4:10

Therefore if any man be in Christ,
he is a new creature: old things are passed away;
behold, all things are become new.
—*2 Corinthians* 5:17

And now abideth faith, hope, charity, these three;
but the greatest of these is charity.
—*1 Corinthians* 13:13

To my Heavenly Father, who gifted me with a love of storytelling and who has walked alongside me every step of the way. And to my faithful readers, who make the ups and downs of writing a book totally worth the journey.

Chapter One

*The honor of your presence is requested
at the marriage of
Corrine Elizabeth Anton
and
Victor Andersen Gyles
Two o'clock in the afternoon
Saturday, October...*

With an exasperated shake of his head, Hayden "Denny" Hunter crammed the summons and RSVP back into the envelope, then tossed it into an open briefcase sitting on the parked Porsche's leather passenger seat. When packing for an unavoidable business trip to "hometown" Hunter Ridge in mountain country Arizona, he'd come across the invitation he'd ignored a few days earlier. So why had he brought it along with him, let alone opened it once he arrived at his destination?

He'd like to believe he was inadvertently added to the invitation list by someone not comprehending the complexity of the situation—that his older stepbrother's betrothed had only in June left Denny standing at the altar, and that after a prolonged absence from the family hotel business, that same stepbrother had also swooped in to carry off a promotion Denny had worked long and hard for.

"At least I *hope*," he said aloud in the confines of his vehicle, "neither Corrine nor Vic chose to be deliberately insensitive."

With a low growl, Denny exited the sports car he'd driven from San Francisco and slammed the door more firmly than necessary. It was a crazy long drive. But although the purpose of this trip on behalf of his mother, Charlotte Gyles, was to have a face-to-face meeting with the manager of an inn she owned, it also gave him a chance to blow the cobwebs out of his brain with a road trip. In particular, it provided uninterrupted time to strategize how to get back in the good graces of his stepfather, hotelier Elden Gyles.

He would fulfill his assignment here—how could he refuse, given his mother's recent car accident?—and tie it to an obligatory visit with his father's side of the family. But he hoped not to linger long in the town he'd set foot in only once since his mother took off with his two-year-old self at the time of his parents' divorce thirty years ago.

He gazed resentfully at the two-story natural stone structure, three guest rooms wide, that had brought him back to this tiny town in the middle of nowhere—the Pinewood Inn. Nor could he help noticing the two vacant buildings his mother owned that abutted it on either side, their boarded-up windows appearing as unseeing eyes that faced the winding, ponderosa pine–lined main road through town.

That had creeped him out as a kid two decades ago. Kind of did now, too.

"Hey, Mister." A soft, childish voice came from the shadowed recesses of the inn's broad porch. "Do you want to buy a ticket to the Hunter's Hideaway Labor Day charity barbecue?"

No, he did not. He wanted to take care of business and get himself back home before his stepbrother—five years his senior—commandeered more than what he'd already laid claim to.

The child who'd delivered the sales pitch jumped up from a rocking chair where she'd been sitting and cautiously moved to the railing, a brown envelope clutched to her chest. Slanting rays of a late August sun illuminated a blond-haired, freckle-faced girl not much older than seven or eight. She wore jeans and a turquoise knit top, and her solemn eyes reflected a wariness that belied the courage it must have taken for her to speak to a stranger.

He offered the girl a reassuring smile. "Sure, I'll buy one."

Her eyes widened. "You will?"

He must be her first customer. "How much?"

"Twenty dollars."

Giving a low whistle, he pulled out his wallet, remembering the five dollars his dad had grudgingly forked over for a similar event the first—and only—time a then-twelve-year-old Denny had come for a visit. Inflation had hit even here in the backwoods, but no doubt it was for a worthy cause—and there was no obligation to attend. He'd be long gone by the weekend.

"Here you go." He held out the requested amount as the girl joined him on the sidewalk.

Brows lowered in sober concentration, the youngster tucked the bill into the envelope, then carefully extracted a printed ticket and handed it to him. "See that number? You can win a prize."

"Can't beat a deal like that, can I?"

"Nope."

"What else do you say, Taylor?" a pleasant female voice called from behind them.

He and the miniature charmer looked to where a woman in her late twenties approached, dark waves of collar-length hair glinting in the sunlight and her high-heeled pumps tapping rhythmically on the sidewalk. Her black pencil skirt that hit just above the knees, pink top and gray blazer seemed out of place for a Monday afternoon in this laid-back little town. Nevertheless, she was an eye-catcher.

The girl she'd called Taylor obediently looked up at him. "Thank you, mister."

Still no smile.

"You're welcome. I'm sure a pretty girl like you will sell a lot of tickets." The disbelieving look she returned nearly made him pull out his wallet a second time and buy ten more.

The woman—Taylor's mother?—gazed affectionately at the youngster, then dipped her head to study him over the top of tortoiseshell-rimmed glasses, revealing the most beautiful hazel eyes he'd ever seen.

"Are you here to see about a room?" Those amazing eyes brightened expectantly. "We do have a vacancy."

She worked at the inn?

"Actually, I'm here to see the inn's manager, Miss Everett." Formerly the community library manager, the older woman had befriended his mother decades ago, when as a newlywed his parent struggled with the isolation of the town and a marriage that was far from what she'd dreamed of.

The brunette tilted her head. "Viola Everett is my great-aunt. I'm Lillian Keene. And you are…?"

"Charlotte Gyles's son." Her eyes widened slightly, confirming she recognized his mother's name. Was this the niece his mother said had cared for Miss Everett when she'd broken a hip last winter? "I'm Hayden Hunter."

Inwardly he winced, recalling the wedding-day text message he'd received while standing at the front of a church sanctuary, all eyes on him. *You are a hard man to love, Hayden Harrison Hunter.* "But I prefer Denny. Or Den."

He shook her offered hand, not caring for the unwelcome spark of awareness that shot through him at her touch. If there was one thing he didn't need right now, it was being attracted to a woman who might all too soon wish she'd never laid eyes on him.

Her smooth forehead creased. "One of the Hunter's Hideaway Hunters."

"More or less." But unlike most of his half siblings and cousins on his dad's side, his parents' divorce and his early exit from Hunter Ridge ensured he hadn't played a part in the family legacy in this region. Hunter's Hideaway was one of the holdings of the family-run Hunter Enterprises, a business catering to hunters, hikers, horsemen and other outdoor enthusiasts. "I grew up in San Francisco. Live there now."

Her smile widened, catching him off guard. "In that case, I especially thank you for coming all this way. It's greatly appreciated."

Appreciated? Surely his mother hadn't given her the impression she was having him drop in for a cup of coffee and a friendly chat. Shifting uncomfortably, he smiled down at the little girl who gazed at him with open interest, then winked at her—and for the first time glimpsed a shy smile.

"Your daughter is quite the salesperson. I came close to buying her entire stock of tickets."

"I'm not her daughter." The child shot him an insulted glare.

"Taylor's my niece." Lillian reached out to draw the girl to her side, but, as if sensing her intention, Taylor abruptly knelt to inspect a fist-size pinecone on the sidewalk. What he interpreted as hurt momentarily clouded the woman's lovely eyes. "She's staying with me for a while."

Apparently having had enough of adult company, Taylor handed her aunt the envelope, then hopped up on the porch and disappeared inside the building.

But even without the child's listening ears, he didn't intend to conduct business where passersby might be privy to his mother's and the inn manager's affairs. One young couple had already paused to give his silver Porsche an admiring once-over. He should have driven something less conspicuous, but too late now.

He motioned to the inn. "Perhaps we should step inside?"

"Yes, please come in." Delivering another smile that ramped his heart rate up a notch, she turned to the inn and tilted her head in invitation for him to follow. "My aunt will want to meet you, and I know you're tired from the drive and could use some refreshment. I'm grateful Mrs. Gyles sent someone in response to our inquiries."

Interesting way of putting it. Constant complaints was more like it. Demands for plumbing fixes, gutter and downspout repairs, appliance and flooring replacements. Window treatments, furnishings and other upgrades. His mother, dealing with grueling postaccident physical-therapy challenges, had persuaded him to personally address the situation. No doubt she thought a son who'd spent the last decade directing renovation and management of properties for his stepfather's boutique hotel enterprise, GylesStyle Inns, could best evaluate the complaints.

She wanted him to determine the level of attention the inn realistically required—superficial only, a moderate renovation or an investment in "the works." Or, considering the possibility of Miss Everett's deteriorating health—which he was also asked to report back on—was it best to shut down the inn and be done with it?

Denny was all for the latter.

But as he stepped onto the porch where Lillian Keene awaited him, he couldn't help but notice that the paint on the white railing and wooden door was chipped and the porch's floorboards were in need of resealing. Maybe those complaints were legitimate?

He frowned. "Ms. Keene, what—?"

"Lillian, please." She opened the door and entered the shadowy interior. He followed, noting the welcoming creak of a hardwood floor and the faint scent of furniture oil.

"I'm especially grateful," she continued, "that Mrs. Gyles is willing to see to the repairs before my aunt's contract renews. We've been concerned as to the inn's long-term sustainability in its current condition. Thanks in part to your mother's efforts to draw an artisan dynamic to the town, guest expectations are rising. No criticism intended—tastes do change over time—but who knows when the most recent interior-design decisions were made? Obviously sometime after the structure was built by my great-great-grandfather in 1927, so it's long overdue for a freshening up in multiple respects. And do you think there's something your mother can do about those boarded-up buildings next door? Such an eyesore."

Staring at her, Denny felt a muscle in his stomach tighten. Had his mother forgotten to call ahead as she'd promised? She was supposed to pave the way for his visit.

A quick glance around the entryway and into the spacious front parlor confirmed they were alone, but he lowered his voice.

"Actually, Ms. Keene… Lillian…" His mother had been clear about his marching orders. "I was asked to come here for what, depending on my findings, may result in something else altogether."

"And what would that be?"

He shouldn't be discussing his mother's business with anyone other than Viola Everett, but no doubt the condition of the building, her aunt's health and subsequent ability to perform her job well were fair topics for this niece who was evidently so involved with the inn.

"I'm here to let your aunt know," he said as gently as he could, "that depending on my evaluation of the property, her managerial contract may not be renewed. The inn may be closed."

Please, God, this can't be happening.

But it was. And it was *her* fault.

Heart pounding, Lillian took in Hayden Hunter's somewhat road-weary sea-blue eyes and dark brown, neatly styled hair. He was solidly built—a navy golf shirt emphasized broad shoulders, and charcoal Dockers showed off slim hips. A scar nicked the corner of his mouth, and the

firm jaw was in need of a shave this late in the day. But
now she couldn't believe she'd thought him story-worthy
handsome when she'd first spied him talking to Taylor.

With an agenda like his, he was no storybook hero.

"Charlotte is considering closing the Pinewood Inn?"
Her words came out more sharply than intended. "Why?
Because my aunt spoke up for her own best interests and
those of your mother? Tried to persuade her that much-
needed upgrades to the property are overdue?"

A flicker of surprise, followed by a slight narrowing
of his eyes, confirmed Denny had been taken aback by
her heated response. And didn't like it.

"What is your connection to the inn? Other than that
it's managed by Viola Everett, who happens to be your
great-aunt. Are you employed here?"

"No, I'm not an employee. I'm…"

What was she? A Phoenix librarian by profession.
Then when her single aunt had faced serious medical
obstacles in January with a fall that broke a hip, she'd
taken a leave of absence to care for her. After a series of
personal setbacks of her own, she'd ended up staying on,
assuming the day-to-day management of the inn around
part-time library clerk employment. A position that, God
willing, might soon open up to a full-time one.

Hunter Ridge not only was her aunt's lifelong home,
but was more conducive to meeting the needs of Lillian's
troubled niece—for however long Taylor remained with
her this time. Both great-aunt and niece, however, would
have to pack up and go with her to Phoenix if she was unable to support them here. Unfortunately, relating those
personal details to Denny Hunter wouldn't prove her va-
lidity to speak on her aunt's behalf that he was seeking.

"I believe, Ms. Keene—" A faint smile touched his

lips. No more *Lillian*. "—that I should speak directly with your aunt regarding business matters going forward."

"But I'm—" *Don't go there. Don't further sink your aunt's ship by implying she's no longer capable of running the operation on her own.* "My aunt would be entirely comfortable with my participation in conversations regarding her role and the future of the inn."

He shrugged. "If she's agreeable, I'll continue this conversation with both of you."

"Then I'll let her know you're here." Lillian's smile evaporated as she headed to the rear of the inn.

Your fault. Your fault. Your fault.

Knowing what she did from Aunt Viola about Charlotte Gyles and her history of animosity toward Hunter Ridge, why had she encouraged her aunt to email her employer with what might be interpreted as demands? In fact, her aunt had balked at emailing the requests, but Lillian had been persistent, naively placing confidence in the fact that Mrs. Gyles—formerly Mrs. Douglas Hunter of Hunter Ridge—held her aunt in high regard. Hadn't she, in many respects, indulged Aunt Viola in allowing her to manage the inn when she'd retired from her librarian position?

Lillian hadn't expected a backlash.

The kitchen and dining room were empty of both aunt and guests, so she let herself into the two-bedroom apartment she and Taylor currently shared with the inn's manager.

The little girl was sprawled on a floral love seat, her nose buried in a book, and Lillian's heart contracted at her resemblance to Lillian's younger sister, Annalise. Slim build. An upturned nose. Long-lashed green eyes that reflected a wary fragileness not often seen in a child her age.

But was that any surprise?

Her mother, red-eyed and sniffling, had dropped her daughter off on the first day of June, whispering that she needed time to breathe. To live life apart from the never-ending responsibility of child-rearing. She had a new man in her life—of course. And right then and there, she handed off Taylor's overstuffed suitcase, gave her bewildered daughter a hug and drove away.

Again.

The look Taylor gave Lillian as she entered the apartment and placed the ticket envelope on the table was anything but welcoming. That was a familiar pattern that always followed when the child's mother put in an unexpected appearance. In a few days, however, Taylor would recover from her mom's visit Saturday, and all would be well again—or fairly well—between aunt and niece.

Drop off. Visit. Reclaim. Drop off. Visit. Reclaim.

How long would it be before Annalise again tired of the latest man in her life and bounded back into Taylor's, sweeping her from Lillian's arms and away from a stable home? Annalise wasn't a bad person, but she was immature and too often thought solely of herself. Was Lillian morally obligated to try to gain legal custody? Or was she fooling herself that if given the opportunity she could eventually break down the walls her niece had built around her heart, which had her pulling away when anyone got too close.

Shortly after Taylor's arrival, Lillian had guiltily consulted a lawyer. But he'd warned that with her being a single woman, currently working part-time and in temporary housing with an elderly aunt, she didn't have much to prove that her situation was superior to her sister's. And now, if the inn closed, they'd lose the roof over their heads until other arrangements could be made. So things would look worse than ever, should she attempt to take legal action now.

"Is Aunt Viola here, Taylor?"

Focused again on the book, she didn't look up. "Nap."

That extreme weariness was one of the reasons Lillian continued to stay on with an aunt who'd always welcomed her for visits when as a child and adolescent Lillian needed an anchor in the storm of her parents' seminomadic lifestyle. An anchor against which Annalise chose to rebel.

As much as Lillian wanted to continue the discussion with Denny, however, she wouldn't wake her aunt. She'd be groggy. Not at her best. Not how Lillian wanted Charlotte Gyles's son to see her. With a regretful glance at Taylor, she stepped back into the hallway and pulled the door shut. Then, mustering what she hoped was a convincing smile, she returned to the front of the inn, where she'd left Mr. Hunter.

In her absence, he'd moved from the entryway into the front parlor and was inspecting the fireplace. Had he checked out the crack in the window? The drapery rod pulling loose from the wall and the water stain on the ceiling? What were his qualifications, anyway, to be "evaluating" the inn?

And judging her aunt.

Unfortunately, the latter was what he was undoubtedly here for as much as anything. To report back to his mother that her aging friend was no longer capable of fulfilling her responsibilities. The condition of the property was a secondary issue.

Sensing her presence, the man turned in her direction with an easy smile, his brows lifted in expectation.

"I'm afraid my aunt's unable to join us at the moment. If you'd care to wait…?" *Please, please don't let him wait, Lord.*

"As a matter of fact—" He glanced at his watch. "I'm joining my father shortly and need to check into my cabin at the Hideaway first. I got to town early and thought I'd stop in to introduce myself. I didn't plan to inspect the property today."

Did he expect her to thank him for that? Truth of the matter was that he'd hoped to catch them off guard. Wouldn't he have otherwise called ahead for an appointment?

"You'll return tomorrow, then? Say ten a.m.?" She wasn't working at the library Tuesday, and her aunt would be at her best to meet him in the morning, so she may as well call a few shots here. Control what she could.

"Ten it is."

He thrust out his hand, and she reluctantly shook it, irritated at the way his larger one engulfed hers and sent a betraying tingle racing up her arm. *He's nice enough to look at, but don't make the same mistake twice.*

For a fleeting moment their gazes locked, questioning, as if seeking to draw out the secrets the other harbored. Then he released her hand and headed out the door.

Intending to follow him onto the porch, she abruptly halted at the threshold, loath to step out on the street where teenager Randy Gray was ogling Denny Hunter's shiny sports car. Her face heated. Not a single time since she'd left Cameron Gray standing at the altar in June had his younger brother failed to greet her with flapping wings and clucking chicken sounds.

She stepped farther back into the shadowed interior. But too late. The blond fourteen-year-old had glimpsed her and, fists curled under his armpits, he strutted slowly around the back of the car, his head bobbing. The toe of his tennis shoe scratched at the blacktop surface. A cluck. A squawk. Then he threw back his head with a yelping laugh and raced off down the street.

A bewildered-looking Denny glanced back at her.

She held up her hands in a beats-me gesture. "What can I say? Small-town eccentricity. Get used to it."

Eccentric or not, though, she'd stay inside until certain Cameron's brother wasn't circling back. She had to prepare her aunt for what might be coming—and to decide what they were going to do about it if worse came to worst.

Chapter Two

"As much as I don't look forward to this," Denny mumbled under his breath when he pulled his car up outside the inn shortly before ten o'clock Tuesday morning, "it can't be any worse than dinner with Dad last night."

Like oil and water, he and Doug Hunter had clashed throughout the meal. That wasn't surprising, considering it was his dad who'd long ago told him he wasn't an easy kid to love. Maybe he wasn't, but being respected trumped being loved any day in Denny's book. And while they'd seen each other intermittently through the years—the last time being when Dad witnessed Denny's recent wedding fiasco, which, thankfully, wasn't mentioned during dinner—he didn't have much hope they'd ever be close.

To Denny's relief, his grown half siblings and their spouses hadn't joined them for the meal, and Vickie, his dad's second wife, excused herself to attend a Bible study group before her husband got revved up to launch in on the sins of Charlotte Gyles. Not surprisingly, what his father related didn't jibe with the story Denny's mother told as to what brought about the demise of their relationship—and her acquisition of well over a half dozen of his inherited Hunter Ridge properties in a divorce settlement. Full custody of Denny, too. More than a few other never-before-heard twists were thrown in. And although he did his best to listen to Doug Hunter rant as he made sure his son "got the truth of it," Denny wasn't going to get caught in the middle of a domestic brouhaha that nobody had settled after three decades.

Get over it, Dad.

Considering the example his parents set for matrimony, it's a wonder he'd ever garnered the courage to ask Corrine to marry him. Then again, she had her own baggage to deal with and her own reasons for accepting his proposal.

Her own reasons for publicly dumping him, as well.

But he wasn't going to think about that now.

He'd just stepped out of the car when his phone vibrated. As he paced the sidewalk in front of the inn, his assistant, Betsy, filled him in on what had transpired at the office since his departure. His stepbrother, Vic— brand-new VP of operations—had stopped by looking for him. He'd loitered awhile in Denny's office with the door closed, then left.

Not good.

With an uneasy feeling, he wrapped up the call, tucked his phone away and then stepped up on the porch just as the front door opened. There stood a plump, silver-haired older woman dressed in a dark green paisley-print dress. Considering what his mother had shared about Miss Everett's health issues, he'd expected a more fragile-seeming woman than the one before him.

She smiled. And although they were likely close to

five decades apart, he could see a faint family resemblance to Lillian in that smile.

"Miss Everett, I'm Denny Hunter, Charlotte's son."

The corners of her eyes crinkled as she nodded knowingly. "I remember you."

Remembered him? Perhaps the downturn in health wasn't solely a physical one?

Lillian appeared behind her aunt, more casually dressed today in a denim skirt and a scoop-neck blue top. She was every bit as pretty as the day before. "Aunt Viola tells me you were in her Toddler Twos class at Sunday school."

His mother had taken him to church? He had no recollection of that. To his knowledge, he'd only set foot in a church for weddings and funerals.

"My, my, yes," the older woman continued as she studied him. Was she looking for similarities between him and his mother? His father? "You were a cute little guy. Chubby. All serious. But you loved the puppet stories. Especially David and Goliath."

He shook his head. "I wish I shared those memories."

"I'll see if I can find photos. I always took pictures of my classes."

"Let's not leave Denny standing out here on the porch, Aunt Viola."

Lillian offered him a slightly warmer smile than the one he'd departed with yesterday. It had been obvious she hadn't taken his visit well, but she seemed to have recovered her poise and had no doubt by now enlightened her aunt as to the purpose of his trip to Hunter Ridge. Hopefully that had given the older woman an opportunity to absorb it. Come to terms with the possibilities.

"Please come in," Lillian added. "What do you want us to show you first?"

He'd much rather be left to poke around on his own, but this was Viola's home as well as an inn his mother owned, and he should respect that.

"Lillian tells me," Viola said, as they moved through the entryway and into the parlor, "that after reviewing our recommendations, Charlotte has concerns about investing in upgrades to the property. That she may choose instead to permanently close the inn."

"That's certainly an option on the table, yes." One that he'd do his best to get his mother to see the wisdom of. He'd perused the accounting ledger of income and expenses before his trip, and the operation here wasn't much more than a break-even proposition. He was surprised his stepfather hadn't discouraged her from throwing away more money on it. Then again, Elden Gyles adored Denny's mother. Doted on her. Indulged her. Which, according to Denny's father, had played a part in the breakup of his parents' marriage.

But while he'd come to the conclusion from afar that the inn was a losing proposition, it didn't seem like it would be easy now to push for a permanent closing in light of meeting Miss Everett face-to-face. The Sunday-school teacher who'd thought him cute would be forced to find a new home and a job elsewhere.

He logged on to his phone and pulled up a list of concerns that he'd gleaned from Viola's emails to his mother. "For starters, why don't you direct me to the items you emailed about? I saw the water stain on the ceiling in this room yesterday. Has the source of the leak been addressed?"

"A toilet upstairs overflowed last spring." Viola shook

her head. "We got a plumber in here to fix that, but not before it did damage down here."

"I noticed the crack in the windowpane, too."

"That's a more recent addition." She rolled her eyes. "Teenagers were throwing a football around in the street during the wee hours of the morning last weekend, and it got away from them."

Teenagers. *Chicken Man?*

Lillian moved to the window and pulled back one of the heavy drapes. "Because the house is old, the window frame has become warped. The repairman suggested it be reframed when he replaces the pane, but that's a greater expense than a single piece of glass, and we'd want the frame to match the other windows, not be a glaring modernism."

He keyed a few notes into his phone, aware that Lillian was watching him closely. No doubt she saw him as a harbinger of doom, swooping into her aunt's quiet, secure world. He was known for his good business sense, decisiveness and an unsentimental eagle eye on the bottom line. That was what people—including his stepfather—counted on him for. Respected him for. But for some reason, it bothered him that those highly regarded traits would be less than admirable to Ms. Keene in this current situation.

"Anything else in here?"

Viola looked to Lillian, who nodded for her to continue. "The electrical outlet on that far wall is dead. There's a buckled floorboard behind the sofa. Wallpaper's pulling loose in places. I keep gluing it, but it won't stay down."

"And the fireplace." Lillian darted a look at him, as if sensing that evidence for closing the inn was mounting. "The flue is cleaned regularly, but it needs serious work both inside and out for safety's sake. When we had it inspected, recommendations were made that we need to follow if we intend to use it this coming autumn."

"Folks do love sitting by a crackling fire on a chilly evening," Viola added. "It lends a homey touch and an excuse for guests to gather around and get to know each other."

He knew that to be true. "Do the guest rooms have fireplaces?"

"A few. But they've long been sealed up."

A mixed bag. He continued to take notes as the issues in this room alone rapidly tallied up. It was more of the same as they progressed through the downstairs. A cozy library. Small office. Spacious dining room. Laundry and storage rooms. Assessing a kitchen featuring weary-looking appliances, cracked floor tile and a chipped sink led to an enjoyable chat in the adjoining breakfast nook with an elderly couple who were finishing up a morning break of fresh fruit and pastries. Viola pointed out the entrance to her apartment, but didn't mention work to be done there or invite him to take a look.

Overall, the house was well cared for. Clean. Neat. But it *was* aging. Neither the somewhat shabby furnishings, heavy and dark with a south-of-the-border feel, nor flooring and wall and window treatments created an appealing ambience that would lure guests back for a second visit. He hadn't seen the upstairs rooms yet, but clearly the inn required a lot of work, time and money. Three things he couldn't in good conscience encourage his mother to invest in—or willingly agree to oversee himself.

A phone in the office rang, and as Viola went to answer it, he noticed her limp, more pronounced than when he'd first arrived. From the hip broken earlier that year, no doubt. Her cheery demeanor had faded as their route progressed through the inn, giving way to evident weariness. But his presence and known purpose undoubtedly contributed to that. How did his mother expect him to gauge the state of her health? He wasn't a doctor or physical therapist, and he sure couldn't count on her niece for an unbiased opinion. But he had a hard time picturing Viola with the 24/7 energy level that an inn demanded.

Inwardly he cringed when Lillian, perhaps sensing the direction his mind was going, gave him an uncertain smile. Letting her aunt down wasn't going to be easy. Where would a seventy-seven-year-old woman find affordable housing and pick up a monthly paycheck around here? But he couldn't let his mother keep sinking her capital into a money pit like this just to subsidize the life style of someone she'd known while residing here but a few short years. And long ago, at that.

But then Lillian opened the multipaned French doors just off the breakfast room, and they stepped into a walled-in garden.

And everything changed.

Lillian caught a flash of surprise in Denny's eyes as he gazed around the sun-dappled, expansive stone-walled garden.

He glanced at her, his eyes questioning. "This is… unexpected."

"We call it the Secret Garden. We can comfortably seat about thirty-five or forty for a wedding. Fifteen or twenty for a luncheon."

"Nice."

And indeed it was. The perimeter of the one-hundred-foot-deep space featured a variety of trees and bushes and was punctuated by a flagstone walkway leading to a spacious patio that faced a gazebo. Native perennials abounded, skillfully woven in to complement colorful annuals and an occasional stone bench.

"My aunt's green thumb and artistic eye shine the brightest here." Despite a short growing season at this more-than-mile-high elevation, the walls provided a protected microclimate of sorts where greenery flourished, colors and textures changing as the seasons passed. Even wintertime brought to it a stark, pristine beauty. "This gem keeps the Pinewood Inn in the black. It's booked from late spring through midfall for small weddings and receptions, private parties, and luncheons."

"I can see why."

This, in fact, was where her ex-fiancé's sister, Barbie, was to be married in October. Thankfully, despite pressure from the girl's mother, the bride-to-be hadn't held Lillian's runaway-bride act against Aunt Viola or canceled her booking after the aborted June wedding. But the notoriously spoiled young lady was proving to be something of a bridezilla in her demands—which had further spurred Lillian to keep at her aunt to approach her employer for upgrades. It was no secret that the inn itself didn't hold a candle to the romantic draw of the garden. Seldom were guest rooms booked in conjunction with events held there—no bridal-party weekends and certainly no honeymoons or anniversary retreats.

Most repeat guests were those who'd warmed to Aunt Vi's special brand of hospitality, not who craved the more tangible aspects of the inn itself.

Accompanying Denny as he silently wandered the garden walkways, Lillian watched him from the corner of her eye. Did he see what she saw—that the garden deserved guest accommodations to equal it? Maybe something unapologetically romantic, a style more in keeping with the traditional exterior than the blandness that was there now.

"I remember one year an evening Christmastime wedding was hosted here." Her heart lightened at the memory, and she hoped it would touch him, too. "The garden was warmed with decorative patio space heaters, and the pines and bare branches of the deciduous trees were strung with twinkling fairy lights."

She looked to him hopefully. But he was gazing down at his phone and didn't respond. Lillian's stomach knotted when he murmured an apology and stepped away for the third time that morning to take a business call. *So much like Cameron.* He hadn't been able to stay in the moment longer than it took to blink twice, couldn't keep his mind from drifting away to seemingly more important matters. Pity the woman who ended up wed to Hayden Hunter.

Yes, despite her feelings of animosity toward him, she'd checked out his ring finger.

Clearly, though, he wasn't impressed with the Pinewood Inn, and seeing it through his eyes, she couldn't fault him. It hadn't gotten into its current condition overnight. When earlier in the spring she'd criticized her aunt's employer for the neglect, Aunt Viola came to Charlotte's defense, admitting that it was as much her own fault that things had gotten to this stage. Grateful for the opportunity to have a job she enjoyed and a nice place to live postretirement, she'd done her best not to be an albatross around her patron's neck.

"Sorry for the interruption." Denny joined her again, tucking away his phone. "You step out the office door for a few days, and suddenly nobody can live without you."

As was the case with her former fiancé, undoubtedly

that made him feel good about himself. Important. Indispensable.

"As I was saying," she continued, "the winter wedding was lovely, with snow flurries setting a romantic mood for the exchange of vows."

Could he picture that? Or was his mind focused on the drawbacks of the inn and alert to the nuances of her aunt's flagging health? Thankfully, there was no need for a walker or cane this morning. But had he noticed how carefully she turned? How she occasionally gripped the back of a chair or casually leaned against a door frame to steady herself?

Please, Lord, don't let Denny expect Aunt Vi to accompany him to the second floor. Her aunt hadn't navigated the stairs since the fall that broke her hip. Realistically, despite her steady progress, she might never again see those upstairs rooms.

"Your aunt maintains this garden by herself? And manages the inn?" A probing, underlying skepticism seemed to edge his words.

"Mostly." Or at least she had, up until last winter when Lillian had been given a crash course on innkeeping, and later gardening. "Breaking a hip is serious business, and while there are still limitations, she's making remarkable strides."

They were indeed blessed, for she'd read that each year 20 or 30 percent of the several hundred thousand who broke a hip died from the complications within a year. The vast majority never fully recovered, which made Lillian doubly grateful for the steady progress they were seeing.

"My mother will be pleased to hear that."

"She has a housekeeper who comes daily, a woman

who does the laundry, and a few others who fill in when she needs to be away for PT or other reasons. I help as I can." Which ate up all her free time away from the library. "And, of course, she brings in someone to do the heavy work out here. But the garden design is all hers, based on how she recalls her own grandmother kept it. It had deteriorated considerably, of course, by the time Aunt Viola came here. I have before-and-after photos if you'd care to see them."

"That sounds interesting."

But it didn't sound as if it interested *him*.

He tilted his head. "Taylor's in school today?"

What did that have to do with anything? "She is."

"And the two of you live—where?"

That was none of his business. Or would his mother frown on providing free housing to a great-niece and great-great-niece? It had never dawned on her that perhaps their residing here would be unacceptable once her aunt was more mobile. But she still had a long way to go. It was very likely she would never *fully* recover. "For the time being, we share the apartment with my aunt."

"Because…?" He was probably fishing for confirmation that her aunt wasn't fulfilling her duties at the inn.

"Aunt Viola and her sister—my grandmother—were the sole siblings in their family. The inn was sold when Aunt Viola was a young woman, and by the time their parents passed away, my grandma had married and moved elsewhere. Other relatives gradually left town to look for what they thought were better opportunities, as well. That left Aunt Viola on her own. I took a leave of absence after her fall last winter…and stayed on."

He seemed to give that some thought, but she continued before he could misconstrue the situation. "I'm working as a library clerk part-time right now. The current library manager will be retiring soon, and I'm hopeful that as a degreed, experienced librarian, I'll qualify for the position."

However, a few days ago she'd heard rumors that another librarian might be taking early retirement from her job in Denver and would be returning home to Hunter Ridge—to apply for the opening.

"It's commendable you're assisting your aunt." He studied her with evident concern. "But that's a considerable sacrifice for a young woman with her life still ahead of her. Sequestering yourself in a no-prospects, sleepy town like this. I mean, you can only listen to the crickets chirp for so long, right?"

Irritation flared in Lillian. Having spoken like a true city boy, he smiled, confident of his assessment. Counting to ten, she bent to pluck a blanketflower, then twirled the stem between her fingers as she returned his measuring gaze.

"It's not like that at all. I love it here. The beauty of the forest. Knowing your neighbors. Being active in a local church. My parents moved around a lot, so I spent quite a few holidays and vacations here while growing up. In fact, I've never thought of any other place as home. But prior to this year, I never dreamed I might get to live in Hunter Ridge. I'd like to remain here."

"Not what I'd care to do, but to each his own." He offered what could only be taken as a look of commiseration. "I imagine to keep your sanity you make frequent trips to Phoenix? Shopping? Professional sports? Live theater, museums and upscale restaurants? You know, keeping your finger on the pulse of civilization."

If that was his definition of *civilization*, she was happy to do without it.

"Actually, I don't go down there but a few times a year." He probably thought her a dull-as-dishwater bore for admitting that. An unsophisticated bumpkin. Well, let him think whatever he wanted. It didn't much matter to her. "I spent the past decade in the Phoenix area's Valley of the Sun enjoying pleasant winters, palm trees and saguaros, and the extras you mentioned that a metropolis offers. But I endured record-breaking summer heat. Lengthy bumper-to-bumper commutes, scorpions, air-quality alerts and high crime rates. Now I enjoy walking to work, cool summer days and pine-fresh air. I'm looking forward to autumn and hopefully a white Christmas. It seems like a fair trade."

If only she *could* remain here.

If only Mrs. Gyles wouldn't close the inn.

Denny chuckled as she concluded her lengthy sales pitch for mountain country Arizona. "I know my Hunter side of the family has been rooted to this region for over a hundred years. Must be a marker my personal genetic makeup skipped."

"My family has also been rooted here a long time."

He raised a brow. "But in your family's case, everyone except your great-aunt managed to make the great escape."

Did he think closing the inn would be the perfect opportunity for Aunt Viola to flee, as well? To at long last reach the "civilization" she'd missed out on most of her life?

He had no idea the toll that the possibility of closing the inn was taking on her aunt. If the light coming from under her bedroom door last night was an indication, she'd slept little. Her aunt didn't own the inn—although that was an idea they'd explored last evening, only to conclude they didn't have the combined resources required should Denny's mother be persuaded to part with it.

Selling a property she'd acquired when divorcing Denny's father, however, was something Charlotte had done but once. As Aunt Viola recalled, the person she'd sold to—an artist she thought she could trust—immediately resold to her ex-husband and put it back into his hands. So going forward, she chose to lease only—or to let buildings stand vacant and boarded up, a much-resented blight on the community.

Unquestionably, the inn wasn't a big moneymaker, and Mrs. Gyles had every right to close it down when Aunt Viola's contract was up for renewal. Was there *any* way they could convince Charlotte's son that the inn was worth the time and expense involved to make it a viable endeavor?

"Do you think perhaps—?"

But she'd barely started to speak when Denny raised his hand apologetically and stepped away to take another call.

Both disappointed and disgusted, she tossed the flower aside and returned to the inn without giving Hayden Hunter a second glance. She'd just stepped inside and shut the glass-paned doors when she heard someone cry out, followed by what sounded like the crash of breaking dishes.

Her heart in her throat, Lillian rushed to the inn's kitchen to find her aunt tottering on a low step stool in front of an open upper cabinet and staring down at the shattered china. Instantly steadying her, Lillian helped her down.

"What do you think you're doing, Aunt Vi? We agreed months ago that I'd empty the dishwasher and put away the things on the high shelves. You could have fallen."

"Well, I didn't. But I'm so upset about that platter. It was my mother's."

"I loved it, too. But I'm more concerned that could be you down there on the floor if you pull another stunt like that." Lillian gave her a firm look and lowered her voice. "I'll clean this up. I think you should go rest."

"Is *he* still here?"

"Yes."

"And?"

"It's not looking good. But things will look worse if he sees you not at your best. You've made great strides since last winter, and I've been assuring him you're up to speed for renewal of the managerial position. Please don't make me eat my words."

"It's not his decision. It's Char's."

"Well, she sent him, so I assume she trusts his judgment. But in the meantime, please don't risk doing something that could give him further reason to deliver a negative report."

Aunt Viola touched her hand wearily to her forehead. "This is my fault. For breaking my hip. For sending those emails that apparently provoked Char."

"Now stop that. You didn't fall on purpose. And feel free to blame me for the emails. That was my doing. But Mrs. Gyles needed honest communication on the state of things here. Her lack of interest in the property has had you losing business every single day for who knows how long. She needs to step up and take care of things."

"But it's *you* who has to take care of my business. And

take care of me. Taylor, too. That's not right, you giving up your career and—"

"There's nowhere on earth I'd rather be than here with you and Taylor." In fact, in addition to loving the closeness of their crazy mix of a family, she'd discovered a love for innkeeping and gardening that she was just beginning to tap into.

Her aunt's eyes filled with a sadness that tugged at Lillian's heart. "What are we going to do, Lil? If the inn is closed, I mean?"

She had no idea. But she didn't dare let her concerns further upset her aunt. Slipping her arm around her waist, she gave her a squeeze and a rallying smile. "We'll cross that bridge if and when we come to it. And trust God every step of the way. But while we await the verdict, please don't do anything to jeopardize what little hope we do have."

Which didn't appear to be much.

Chapter Three

"So how *is* Viola?" Denny's mother had inquired when he'd stepped away from Lillian to take the call—his parent having first filled him in on the agonies of her physical therapy at the rehab center. The innkeeper's niece had gone inside, giving him some privacy.

"She's holding her own surprisingly well," he said, keeping his voice low as he gazed around his picturesque surroundings and filled his lungs with the rich blend of earth, pine and flowers. It did seem a shame to pull the plug on an events venue like this one. But it couldn't be helped. "The niece you'd mentioned earlier—Lillian Keene—is helping out as Miss Everett continues to recover."

"I didn't know her niece was still there."

"Oh, yes. And if I'm not mistaken, she's the source of the emails you've been badgered with."

"Is there legitimacy to those requests? Viola never said anything about those issues until recently. I was taken off guard."

"They're legitimate." He mentally skimmed through

the lengthy list he'd compiled. "But a good venture to keep pouring money into? Doubtful."

"While the inn's never been profitable, Elden's never once objected, since it's mine from the divorce settlement. He knows Viola was the one person who tried to understand when I was unhappy and confused. Didn't blame me for everything. She was the sole person in town who took the time to get to know me. Who seemed to care."

"But you don't owe her for the rest of her life."

"No, but I hate to see her lose her home at her age, maybe be forced to leave Hunter Ridge altogether."

"Some things can't be helped and, realistically, how many more years do you think she can handle the job?"

"What would it take to fix the place up?"

She hasn't been listening.

With an inward groan, he paced the garden patio. He didn't want his mother underwriting what would likely never amount to more than a fancy rest home for her friend. "I can forward the list to you and ballpark what it might cost. But for a more accurate estimate, I'd have to engage a contractor and touch base with suppliers. That could take considerable time."

Which he did not have to waste.

"Would you do that, Denny?"

Picturing her propped up in her bed at the rehab center, he discerned the wheedling tone she'd used when he was a kid to persuade him to her way of thinking. But he steeled himself.

"Mother, this isn't a good idea. You need to let it go. If you want, I'll look around for housing options for your friend while I'm here. Then you can decide if you want to subsidize those costs. It would be considerably less expensive than what upgrading the Pinewood Inn will be. Much less risky, too."

And take up a lot less of his time, as well.

"But she's always enjoyed the guests, whipping up goodies for them in the kitchen, working in her garden."

Denny stepped into the gazebo and turned to gaze out over the walled space. "I admit it's one amazing garden. But the niece was vague about how much Viola's done with it since her fall, and how much of it she and others have been doing."

"This Lillian seems capable. A hard worker, from what her aunt told me. If there's a chance that with her help Viola could stay there…"

With a sinking feeling, he stared up at the azure sky. It wouldn't kill him to get estimates. Do online window-shopping for an idea of what it would take to revamp the furnishings. No doubt someone once had a bright idea that with Hunter Ridge located in the Southwest, the carved dark wood and paintings of cactus and sunbaked Mexican streets would be suitable. While that might work in a Tucson adobe-style inn, it wasn't cabin-country Hunter Ridge by a long shot. If he had his druthers, he'd go for a more contemporary, streamlined look. A contrast to the traditional exterior.

"I can do the research, but there's no market here for this kind of lodging. People who come up this way stay at outdoorsy places like Hunter's Hideaway."

What did the family's new logo tout? The one he'd seen on their website? Oh, yeah. *Where rustic meets relaxing— without apology.*

"Please, Denny? This would mean so much to me. I know it's never going to be more than a break-even proposition, but…" His mother paused, and he could hear a low male voice in the background on her end, although he couldn't understand the words. "One second. Elden wants to speak to you."

Denny's jaw clenched. His stepfather wanted to speak to him *now*? Where had he been a few weeks ago, before turning the vice-president position over to Vic? Without a word of warning—or of apology afterward.

"Den." The rumbling voice sounded genial enough— but then, that was standard, even when delivering news of budget cuts and severances of contracts with longtime loyal vendors. Denny could picture the sixtysomething hotelier, his salt-and-pepper hair thick and neatly styled, his deceptively casual manner of dress belying that his attire was purchased from top-notch clothiers.

Denny gripped his phone more tightly. "Yes, sir?"

"I understand Char sent you to Arizona to take care of personal business for her."

"With the understanding that I'd be gone from work only a few days." Had his absence not been taken well? "I'm staying on top of business long-distance and will return shortly."

"I'm not concerned about that. But I am concerned that you agreed to see about upgrading a property Charlotte's friend manages, and that it sounds as if you're now unwilling to follow through on that."

A muscle in Denny's throat tightened at the misinterpretation, just as a bird in a nearby tree started into an annoyingly repetitious solo. "What my mother originally asked me to do was evaluate the situation and determine if retaining her ailing friend as manager of the Pinewood Inn and investing a great deal of money in upgrades is a worthwhile option. I did as she asked and confirmed it's a poor investment."

Would that obnoxious bird never shut up?

"You know I'm crazy about your mother, don't you?" Elden never made a secret of that and had always treated her like a queen. Pampered her. In fact, Denny's father blamed his ex's former boyfriend for making her dissatisfied with Hunter Ridge, motherhood and, in particular, her first husband. "I know you care for her, too, Den. So what do you say the two of us get this inn fixed up the way she'd like it? You know how she dotes on that old gal who befriended her in that backwoods hamlet."

Denny stepped out of the gazebo, determined to keep his temper in check. "So you want her to spend a mint on a six-guest-room inn located in the middle of nowhere and hand it over to an old woman who is in questionable health but who also has no training and limited experience in the hospitality field? Pardon me for pointing this out, Elden, but that's not the type of investment you've trained me to make."

"Maybe not, but if you can see to your mother's business and lie low in Arizona while Victor gets acclimated to his new role…" *That's what this is about? Making life comfy for Vic?* "If you can make those things happen, Den, I can make it worth your while."

Denny had heard his stepbrother was struggling—a leader without followers, because most supported Denny stepping into that VP slot. "I'm being banished? Is that what you're telling me?"

His stepfather chuckled. "Not banished. Giving your brother a chance to find his footing without people looking to you for the answers."

"Is that what he's telling you? That I'm trying to undermine him?"

"Apparently you have a loyal following, and that's caused unrest."

"I'm not driving that. It's business as usual, as far as I'm concerned. I'm not stirring up animosity toward Vic."

"That's good to know. But I realize that as long as you're highly visible and available, there are those who may continue turning to you instead of Victor. There seems to be an undercurrent of, shall we say, resentment on the part of some that he was promoted over you."

No foolin'. "Is that surprising? Vic walked out on you and the family business almost a decade ago. Then he waltzes back in—and out of the blue steps into a top spot."

"Although it may seem like it on the surface, it wasn't out of the blue. I told him at the time we had our falling-out that there would always be a place for him in the business."

A place he hadn't earned? A birthright he'd snubbed?

Denny remembered well that blowup between his stepbrother and Elden. It hadn't been pretty, and clearly Elden had been deeply wounded at a betrayal by the offspring he'd poured so much of himself into. That was when Denny set his heart on filling Vic's shoes better than Vic could ever fill them. To earn his stepfather's respect and a leadership role in the family business. He was well on the road to achieving that, until Vic showed up last winter, seemingly humble and contrite…and the tide began to turn.

"From the reaction of others," Denny said carefully as he watched Lillian step out the back door and into the garden, "I think you'd have to agree that expectation wasn't well communicated."

"Come on. He's my son, Den." *And I'm not.* "He's settling down now and is ready to put his nose to the grind-stone. Don't take it personally. You and everyone else knew from the beginning that he is destined for the top spot when I step down. That's still a considerable ways off, but if everyone pulls together, helps him get through this time of transition, it will work out in the long run. For everyone. I'm counting on *you* to make that happen."

Meaning keep out of the way?

"I have responsibilities, projects that I'm in the middle of, people who are depending on me."

Seeking relief from the pressure building inside, his gaze tracked Lillian as she gracefully moved to sit on a shaded stone bench. She was a striking-looking young woman with a country-fresh vivacity that had been absent in the sophisticated, born-to-high-society Corrine. The local librarian seemed considerably less capricious than his former fiancée, too. You wouldn't catch a well-grounded Lillian Keene heading for the hills on *her* wedding day, leaving some poor sucker in the dust.

But as appealing as that small-town allure might be on the surface, it wasn't a girl-next-door type that would help him get ahead at GylesStyle Inns. With the departure of Corrine, he was back to square one. Nevertheless, it was a shame that the pretty Lillian planned to follow in her great-aunt's footsteps and sequester herself in Nowheresville.

"By all means, stay on top of the projects out in the field," Elden responded, drawing Denny's attention again. "But in dealing with others at the home base? Steer them back to Victor and let them learn to depend on him. If you're working on getting this inn fixed up for your mother, that's a good enough reason for stepping back.

No one will question it. You won't have to offer explanations."

Was his stepfather truly that naive? Oblivious to the effort Denny had taken to build a network of strong relationships based on mutual respect as he climbed the corporate ladder? Elden thought his arrogant, self-indulgent son could step in and pick up the reins if Denny laid them down?

Across the garden, Lillian looked up and caught him watching her—those beautiful hazel eyes, even at a distance, almost took his breath away. Nevertheless, he managed to refocus on the conversation at hand.

"And when I've done my time here?" He couldn't help throwing in the prison analogy.

"Then we'll talk. Victor filling that VP opening doesn't mean there isn't still a prime spot for you at GylesStyle—especially if you can keep him and your mother happy."

"And if I can't?"

Silence hung heavy. Except for that irritating bird.

"Well, Den," Elden finally drawled, "see that you do."

From the far side of the garden, with the sound of a merrily trilling robin singing its heart out, Lillian couldn't hear what Denny was saying on the phone. Assuming it was the same call he'd taken before she'd gone inside, it was quite lengthy. His voice remained low and indistinguishable, but from his expression, he didn't like the way things were going.

How often she'd seen that same look of concentration on Cameron Gray's face when he'd returned home to Hunter Ridge in February. Having been let go from a managerial position in Boston, he nevertheless lived on his phone, constantly schmoozing with contacts despite insisting that anyone who remained tied to corporate America was nothing but a fool.

He was at home in Hunter Ridge to stay, he'd declared. Working with his dad at the hardware store, he assured everyone around him that relationships were what mattered. Family. Church. Old friends. This was where he wanted to settle down and raise a family. With *her*. Or so he claimed until the day before their wedding, when he got a call from his former employer—and without consulting her leaped at a job offer, generously volunteering to hire a caregiver for her aunt and to place Taylor at an upscale private school.

Was it any wonder she'd cried and prayed most of the night? The next day, as everyone was gathering for the ceremony, she called the officiating pastor—an out-of-town buddy of Cameron's—to ask him to deliver her no-show news.

Cameron hadn't spoken to her since then, having immediately packed up and left for Boston. Nor had his mother or grandma, even when Lillian removed her personal belongings from the apartment above his parents' garage that the newlyweds intended to call home until they found a place to buy. The two women seemed to find plenty of time to talk *about* her, though, if rumors of their critical remarks regarding her immaturity and heartlessness held any truth. And little brother Randy had made nothing but a nuisance of himself.

At least Cameron's sister, Barbie, caught up in her own autumn wedding plans, didn't seem to care one way or another whether her big brother and Lillian were married happily ever after—or not.

Across the garden, Denny pocketed his phone, then turned in her direction. She stood, determined to make another plea on behalf of the inn.

"Sorry for the interruption. Important call."

"Aren't they always," she said drily, wondering how far she'd get in her appeal before he was again whipping out that cell phone.

He motioned irritably to a Navajo willow in the far corner. "What's with the obnoxious bird, anyway?"

No, that phone call must not have gone well.

She laughed. "Maybe he's happy?"

Denny snorted, then looked at his watch and nodded to the inn. "I guess I should take a look at the guest rooms upstairs."

With Aunt Viola sequestered in the apartment, it didn't take long to go through the second-floor rooms, half of which weren't booked despite a long Labor Day weekend fast approaching. The occupants of the other three were out for the day. Although Denny added items to his lengthy list, he seemed preoccupied, as though something else weighed on his mind. Most telling was the fact that he didn't pull out his phone a single time, not even to check caller ID when she heard it vibrate.

When they reached the bottom of the stairs, she turned to him. "So what do you think?"

"You mentioned earlier you're aware that garden events keep the inn in the black. So you must be at least somewhat acquainted with the business side of things here."

"I kept the books when my aunt was unable to. So, yes, I'm aware that the inn is…holding its own."

"By the skin of its teeth. The Pinewood Inn, sadly, has never been a profitable investment for my mother."

"You're implying that it's been nothing but a charitable endeavor on behalf of Aunt Viola?" That rankled, as Lillian knew how much of herself Aunt Vi had invested in this place trying to keep it going.

"As you know, my mother was struggling to find her place in the world when your great-aunt befriended her. She offered her encouragement, advice and support when many in town extended little sympathy as her marriage fell apart. My mother was a big-city girl, a fish out of water, and undoubtedly she made plenty of mistakes that didn't endear her to others."

"My aunt is a kindhearted woman."

"She is. And deep down, so is my mother. Which is why when Viola retired and asked if she could take over management of the Pinewood Inn, my mother agreed. She was losing money on it anyway—basically kept it open to irritate my father as much as anything. What would it hurt if her dear friend and mentor gave it a try?"

"Aunt Vi did bring it out of the red."

"She did. But it's still not a moneymaker. Never will be."

"We're not asking you to strip the place down to the studs and start from scratch. We're asking that broken things be fixed. Dismal furniture replaced. Peeling wallpaper removed. Bedding and window treatments updated."

"That involves money, time and hard work."

"My aunt and I can provide the hard work." Or at least *she* could. "I understand your concern surrounding the financial issues. That concerns my aunt, as well. But Hunter Ridge is her home. The inn. Her garden. Her guests. I'll personally do anything within my power to enable her to live out the rest of her life, however long that may be, as the inn's manager. For now, this is Taylor's home, too. If your mother makes the requested much-needed changes to the property, I know my aunt can turn it around."

He shook his head. "Maybe, if she had a hospitality degree and decades of experience at other reputable properties to bring to the table... I admit I've seen highly successful enterprises make it under good management in the most unlikely places. But those were spearheaded by professionals with an innate savvy for the hospitality business."

"She may not have a degree, but we've both read every book on innkeeping we can get our hands on. And growing up, I traveled extensively with my parents and know what they liked and didn't like about those brief or extended stays. What *I* liked and didn't like. Aunt Vi traveled in her younger days, too. I strongly believe that kind of personal experience will transfer well here—if the property itself works *for* her and not against her, as it's been doing."

"I admire her—and your—pluck, but it's risky. Successful inns are customarily located in areas that have something to draw people there. Location, location, location, as you've surely heard before."

"Hunter Ridge is rousing itself after that economic downturn a decade or so ago. Your mother's played a role in that—initiating leasing properties to a new artisan dynamic that is taking root and transforming the formerly isolated face of the community. Here at the inn's garden, we've showcased a number of local artists this past summer. It's a market waiting to be tapped into. And if we don't do it, someone else will."

"This garden *is* a prime selling point. But the inn has only six guest rooms available." He gave her a regretful look. "I don't see how that can generate enough return on investment to make it worthwhile."

"So what you're trying to tell me is that you're going to recommend to your mother that she close the inn."

"What I'm trying to tell you is not to get your hopes up that the inn will ever be much more than it is today— even when we've completed the renovations."

Even when...?

She momentarily closed her eyes, gave a slight shake of her head. "I'm sorry, but I'm confused. You are or you are not going to advise your mother that the inn be closed? That my aunt's managerial contract should not be renewed?"

"I've expressed to my mother my professional opinion that the doors to the inn should be closed."

Denny stared into the still-bewildered gaze of the woman standing before him. Saw the hope that had briefly lit her eyes evaporate. She was disappointed in his stance because she truly didn't understand what it took to run a profitable hospitality establishment.

He hadn't been toying with her when pointing out the dismal prospects of the inn and the gloomy odds of making a success of it. He'd only wanted her to clearly understand that the endeavor was a waste of money—his mother's. And a waste of time—*his*. Who was his stepfather, anyway, to insist on throwing good money after bad, just to make his wife "happy"?

And to keep Denny out of the way to give Vic a boost.

Elden had dangled a vague "make it worth your while" carrot in front of him. Then he topped it off with what sounded like an unspoken threat if Vic didn't make a go of things in his new position and if that failure, even in part, could be laid at Denny's doorstep. Like it or not, if he wanted the slimmest chance at a future in a company he'd poured himself into, he'd have to buckle under Elden's demands.

No matter how much it galled.

No matter how unfair it was.

He'd put too much time into GylesStyle Inns to walk away in a snit. If he could pull this project off…there might yet be a future in the family business.

What did he have to lose?

"I explained to my mother exactly what I've explained to you, Lillian. The risk. The unlikelihood of profitability and the preferable route being to shut down the inn." He cleared his throat and steadily met her gaze. "But, regrettably, she disagrees with me."

Lillian remained motionless, expressionless except for the growing glow in her lovely eyes.

"You mean—?"

"I mean I'm acquiescing to my mother's wishes, and despite my personal reservations, the Pinewood Inn will have a second chance."

A gasp escaped her lips.

"Please recognize," he continued, "that I'm not reneging on anything I've said about the inn. I have misgivings. Extreme ones. Make no mistake—I'm not happy about this. But I love my mother and know she genuinely wants your aunt to continue as manager of the Pinewood Inn as long as her health allows."

He'd just have preferred not to be blackmailed by his stepfather to give them this chance.

Chapter Four

"Why don't you run that by Vic, Craig? That falls under his jurisdiction now."

Gazing across the raftered dining room of the Inn at Hunter's Hideaway, where he'd stepped into the lobby away from lunch with Lillian and Viola to take a call, Denny cringed at the profanity-laced grumbling of his colleague and right-hand man.

"I know, I know. But give him a chance. He hasn't been sitting on his thumbs all the years he's been away from GylesStyle. He's stayed active in the hospitality industry, just outside the family fold."

Or so Vic's story went.

With a little encouragement, Denny finally got his colleague pointed in the right direction and off the phone without resorting to the lame excuse that he was busy working on a project for his mother. What he'd wanted to do was provide Craig with the precise answer his friend was seeking. Denny knew it. Would Vic?

This was the first of what would probably be many similar conversations with those in the home office with whom Denny had worked closely.

And it was already killing him.

Back at his table, he again seated himself across from Lillian and her aunt, who were finishing their meal. His, no doubt, was cold. "Sorry. Pressing business. Now, as you were saying, Lillian?"

For a moment he didn't think she intended to respond. That she was irritated at the latest interruption of which she'd borne a similar brunt on several occasions that day. Then to his relief, she glanced at Viola before continuing.

"You've mentioned the need to obtain necessary licensing and permits. Drafting plans and getting estimates. Reinsuring an upgraded property. Aunt Vi and I are wondering when you'll start that. And what the two of us can do to expedite things."

He'd explained over lunch what his background was at GylesStyle, hoping that would give them confidence that he knew what he was doing. Being the son of Charlotte Gyles was far from the only thing he was known for.

"I'm going to get in touch with a Phoenix contractor who saw to—" He halted as both Lillian and Viola, solemn-faced, shook their heads. "What?"

"You're going to bring in an outsider?" Viola's tone was clearly disapproving.

"A whole crew of outsiders, if they're available."

A team he'd worked with in the past had multistate licensing and credentials and would be finishing up a remodel on a GylesStyle Inn in Scottsdale shortly. Maybe he could slip a few weeks into their schedule before they started on their next assignment in Santa Fe. Those guys and gals made some of the HGTV celebs look like amateurs. He needed pros who could get in and get the job done on the Pinewood in record time. Then he'd be free to get back to his real world—assuming Vic didn't sink his ship.

Lillian exchanged a look with her aunt. "You know, Denny, that might not be a good idea."

"Why's that?"

"This isn't a large town," Viola said carefully, as if speaking to a child. "People will expect us to engage workers locally, or at least from neighboring towns here in the high country."

"Going elsewhere will cause hard feelings," Lillian clarified. "That's something we can't afford to do. Many of those who for years have engaged the garden for special events are local builders, plumbers, electricians and painters."

Viola nodded.

"Well, ladies, I understand your concerns. But as nice as it would be to accommodate the locals, we need a cohesive, experienced team that can get in here and take care of business in one fell swoop."

Both women again exchanged a look, then shook their heads in unison.

He could almost feel his blood pressure rising as they stared him down. He didn't have the time to vet and individually contract the people needed. It would be like herding cats. And trust a local contractor to do it? No way would he bring in workers from a dinky town for a project like this. "Look, ladies…"

"You may as well shut the place down, then, young man." Viola pushed her empty plate away. "People here need the work and won't be forgiving if we move ahead in hopes of feathering our own nest at the expense of theirs."

"We do have good craftsmen in the region." Lillian

folded her napkin and placed it on the table. "Hunter Ridge. Show Low. Pinetop-Lakeside. Canyon Springs."

That was well and good, but he had no idea of the speed or caliber of those people's work or the quality of their suppliers. Or if they'd even be available. Too much was at stake if he neglected his GylesStyle responsibilities for long. He did *not* intend to get down in the weeds on this project to keep his mother happy.

Well, Den, see that you do.

He darted a look at Lillian and her aunt, hoping he hadn't groaned aloud as his stepfather's words echoed painfully through his brain.

He took a steadying breath, unwilling to throw in the towel. "Believe me, I understand your concerns, but I'm here a limited time. I have responsibilities elsewhere. I need to have a team I can trust to get in and get the job done right. The faster that happens, the quicker you can start filling up those empty rooms."

"Todd Samuels is a top-notch contractor." Viola's gaze lingered on her niece, and if Denny wasn't mistaken, pink rose in Lillian's cheeks. "He has a good bunch working with him."

"And that guy who ramrodded the remodel on Hunter Ridge Wild Game Supply last year. Ted?" Lillian turned to Denny with a hopeful smile. "Your cousin Grady can vouch for him."

Viola gave a firm nod. "Kent Hewdon rewired the whole church a few years back, too, remember? Everyone said he did a fine job of bringing it into the twenty-first century. And don't forget Penny Lund and her sisters painted the interior of Rusty's Grill last month. They did that fancy texturing and everything. They have their own company and often work with Todd. Real pros."

"What I have in mind, though," Denny jumped in, "are people experienced with hospitality property renovations. I imagine the game supply and the restaurant, the church, all turned out fine. But—"

"Well, look who's here!" a male voice boomed. "Lily the librarian. I haven't seen you in months, you pretty little thing."

Color tinged Lillian's cheeks as a big burly guy about Denny's age leaned down to give her a hug. Dressed in outdoor work clothes, the man gave Viola a gentle hug, too, then thrust out his hand to Denny.

"Todd Samuels. Sorry for barging in on your lunch."

Denny shook his hand. But he instantly didn't like him. Didn't think he was sorry, either.

Still flushed, Lillian turned to Denny, the color in her cheeks deepening when she caught him watching her. Were those two an item? Or maybe the pushy guy was hoping to be?

"Todd, this is Denny Hunter." Then she motioned to the newcomer almost apologetically. "Todd used to live in Hunter Ridge and lives in a neighboring town now, so we don't get to see each other often."

His choice or hers?

"Hunter, huh?" Todd's forehead crinkled. "I know most of the Hunters around here. Don't recall a Denny."

"I didn't grow up here. San Francisco."

Todd jerked his head toward the front of the inn. "That piece of junk parked out there with the California plates is yours, I suppose?"

"It is."

Todd squinted one eye. "How's it ride?"

"Smooth as silk."

Giving a low, envious whistle, he nudged Lillian's

arm. "Don't you go letting this city slicker spoil you, Lily. A Ford F-150 is the Cadillac of choice for this part of the country."

Lillian blushed again. "Denny's mother owns the Pinewood, and he's here to see about renovating it."

"No foolin'? About time."

"We need a contractor," Viola piped up, avoiding Denny's gaze. "Know a good one?"

The man laughed, then turned again to Denny. "Seriously? You need a contractor?"

"We haven't gotten that far yet. We're in the preliminary stages of planning and—"

He faltered as Viola shot him a dirty look of a caliber he'd never have expected from a woman of her age and otherwise pleasant disposition.

"Yes, he needs a contractor," she confirmed. "Lil and I don't want him bringing in a bunch of outsiders."

Todd shook his head. "Nope. Don't need that around here. My crew's finishing up a project in Show Low. What's your timeline on this?"

"That hasn't been established yet. I'm—"

"In a hurry." Viola rapped her knuckles on the table. "We need the work done ASAP. Before Barbie Gray's wedding."

Who was Barbie Gray?

Todd folded his arms and gave Denny an assessing look. "So what are we talking here? Strictly cosmetic touch-ups? Repairs or a full face- and body lift?"

"The works," Viola added.

"Now, we don't know that yet." Lillian touched her lightly on the arm as she darted a look in Denny's direction. "That's up to Denny."

Viola nodded at Todd. "*And* his contractor."

Denny held up his hand. "Let's not get ahead of ourselves, Viola. We're just getting started."

"You were the one who said you can't stay long. Have stuff you gotta get back to in the big city. Don't pray for stuff and then refuse it when the good Lord puts it right in front of your face."

He didn't remember praying at all, but if it would help him curb this conversation that was spiraling out of control, he might have to start.

Perhaps sensing his mounting frustration, Lillian turned to her aunt. "Now, Aunt Vi, Denny only finished his inspection of the house an hour or so ago."

Her aunt smirked. "God works fast, doesn't He?"

Todd wisely suppressed a grin as Lillian focused her attention again on Denny.

"I imagine you need to review your notes. Determine the direction you want to go."

He jumped at the lifeline she'd thrown him. "That's right. Still a lot to do, including finding out what kind of budget we'll be working with."

Todd pulled a business card from his shirt's front pocket and handed it to him. "Keep me in mind when you're ready to rock and roll."

Don't count on it, bucko.

Denny stood and the two men shook hands again. Then Viola pushed back her chair as Todd headed off to join a couple of men at another table.

Viola's regretful gaze followed. "If we're not making decisions today, I need to get back to the inn. Tyra's covering for me, but I don't want to take advantage."

"Guess that means me, too, since I drove." Lillian smiled as she got up and helped her aunt to her feet.

"Thank you for meeting with me, ladies." He'd felt

obligated to treat them to lunch after his morning evaluation of the property carried into the noon hour.

"And thank you for lunch, young man. But do remember, don't be calling on God and begging for things you don't plan to take Him up on. That's kinda like crying wolf, and it could work against you. God won't know when you're serious and when you're not."

"I'll keep that in mind."

Viola moved ahead without Lillian's further assistance, and her niece smiled apologetically before following in her wake.

He looked down at his hamburger and fries. Both were definitely cold. Then he flagged down a waitress for a carryout box and paid the bill. Surprisingly, he'd been in Hunter Ridge just short of twenty-four hours and hadn't seen anyone he knew except his dad and Vickie. He'd kind of expected, when word got around of his being in town, that there might be some kind of larger family get-together. A dinner. Dessert. Coffee at the very least.

Something.

Then again, as he recalled from that last visit, he got the impression Charlotte Gyles wasn't that well thought of around here. His Hunter cousins had made it clear that opinion extended to him. In fact, he owed one of them, Garrett McCrae, a black eye. But he supposed it was too late to collect on that one now that he'd heard the guy was, of all things, the pastor of Christ's Church of Hunter Ridge. Go figure.

In the lobby, he paused to pick up a real-estate flyer from a bin, noting that while her aunt had apparently gone on out to the car alone, Lillian lingered, visiting with the gal at the reservations desk.

He'd just reached the exit himself, intent on getting

back to his cabin and making a few phone calls, when his dad came in the door, obviously surprised to see him standing there.

As Denny stepped back, his father pulled his Western hat from his head and squinted one eye. "I got caught up in other things at dinner last night," he said in his usual bold tone, "and failed to express my condolences."

"Condolences?" Confused, Denny shook his head, catching the concerned gaze of Lillian Keene from where she still chatted with the clerk.

"Yeah." His dad cleared his throat, obviously uncomfortable. "You know, for getting dumped at the altar by that society chick."

Denny's face heated as his gaze again collided with Lillian's. Then she quickly looked away.

She heard.

Great. Just great.

If things hadn't changed since his mother lived here—and he was pretty sure they hadn't—by breakfast tomorrow, that bit of humiliating news would have made the rounds of the mighty metropolis of Hunter Ridge.

Lillian slipped out the library door at a quarter after five the next day and started down the storefront-lined street toward the inn, where she and her aunt were to meet with Denny. He wanted to discuss his vision for the property, and she had ideas, too—notes and magazine photos tucked in her tote bag.

But here she was, having practically begged Denny to give them a chance to redeem the inn, and she discovered he'd recently been jilted—the humiliation of it clearly written in his eyes when his dad had publicly expressed his sympathy. If Denny found out she'd left Cameron Gray at the altar, any slight favor he was inclined to do for her and her aunt would likely go down the tubes.

"Hey, Lillian. Pretty outfit."

"Thanks, Packy." She smiled as she passed by a bearded, bald ex-marine who was placing a dinnertime specials display outside his Log Cabin Café. Had she overdressed today, knowing she'd be meeting with Denny Hunter after work? Surely the knee-length gray skirt, white knit top and turquoise sweater she'd flung over her shoulders weren't out of the ordinary. But this morning she *had* impulsively discarded her standard workday pumps for a strappy pair of dress sandals. Because she felt like it, right? Not because she was trying to catch the attention of anyone.

Especially not Denny, who hadn't pretended to be pleased with his mother's decision to accommodate Aunt Vi. He was being decent enough about it and nice to her aunt, at least on the surface. But as she well knew, men could change in an instant and offer no apologies.

Thankfully, today Cameron's brother wasn't lurking about on the streets to mock her as she passed. But if Denny remained in Hunter Ridge for any length of time, it wouldn't be long before he'd hear the gossip. You don't dump one of the town's favorite sons and walk away unscathed, despite the fact that you'd made the right decision. But right decision or not, how could she ever trust herself again to know when she'd truly found "the one" God intended?

Assuming He had one lined up for her.

"Hi, Lillian!" Town council member Sunshine Carston Hunter waved from the entrance to the Hunter Ridge Artists' Cooperative that she managed. "It's been such a gorgeous day, hasn't it?"

"Perfect."

Since walking down the aisle last Valentine's Day with Denny's cousin Grady, her artist friend's spirits always seemed upbeat. Every day better than the last. Lillian gave a little sigh as she continued on down the street. While marriage seemed to suit her friend, Lillian didn't regret not marrying Cameron. In hindsight, though, maybe she could have handled it differently. Less publicly. But then again, he'd blindsided her. Refused to *listen*.

No doubt Denny Hunter's former fiancée had good reason to make an abrupt escape, too. Women didn't do something like that on a whim.

Up ahead his Porsche glinted in the sun, as out of place on the streets of Hunter Ridge as you could get. Last night Aunt Viola had filled her in on what she remembered of Denny's parents' breakup when he was a toddler. Rough start for a kid, but with Charlotte Hunter marrying hotelier Elden Gyles not long afterward, her son appeared to have had a privileged upbringing and landed squarely on his feet.

She checked on her aunt and Taylor, then found Denny in the dining room, an oversize pad of blue-squared graph paper on the table before him, along with a tape measure and ruler. And, of course, his ever-present cell phone an arm's length away. He was dressed more casually today in jeans and a black T-shirt, but that in no way diminished the in-command energy he exuded—and that she reluctantly admired.

It was a wonder, though, that he was willing to include her aunt in today's meeting, considering how she'd brazenly tried to pin him down on hiring Todd as his contractor yesterday. After Cameron's departure in June,

Aunt Vi had gotten it in her head that Todd, the grandson of a friend of hers, should be the man of her niece's
dreams. Had either Denny or Todd grasped her aunt's
underlying motive?

Denny looked up to see Lillian standing in the doorway, an unexpected smile breaking through an expression
of intense concentration while marking something on
the paper. Inexplicably, her breath caught as she was reminded of her first impression of the man she'd glimpsed
chatting with Taylor two days ago—before she knew
what he was doing here.

"Aunt Vi will be a little late. She's on the phone with
a friend."

He nodded, then pointed with his mechanical pencil.
"Floor plan. A rough one, anyway."

She moved to stand by him and gazed down at his
day's work, then lifted the top sheet to look at the second-
floor specs. "Wow. This took a lot of time."

He looked pleased that she recognized that. "It took
hours to measure the rooms, and typical of old structures
like this one, the wall measurements don't always line
up the way you expect them to."

Her gaze swept the walls of the dining room. "There
are gaps? Empty spaces? So there *could* be truth to an
old story that the Newell family treasure is hidden here
somewhere?"

He cast her a dubious look. "Family treasure?"

She set her tote bag on one of the dining chairs. "According to Aunt Viola, anyway."

"What kind of treasure are we talking about? Gold
doubloons? Chest of jewels? A plastic ring from a Happy
Meal?"

She laughed. "That's just it. My aunt doesn't know.

She remembers her mother talking about it sometime after the family sold the place when Aunt Vi was away at college. She remembers her saying it was a shame that it had never been found—something that her grandpa Benjamin Newell had hidden here—and that in selling, they'd lose the opportunity to keep looking for it."

"Then your aunt, in essence, regained the opportunity when she started managing the inn."

"And she's been looking off and on for whatever it is for well over a dozen years. For something my great-great-grandfather, who built this place, was supposed to have stashed for safekeeping."

"Intriguing."

But she could tell he didn't think there was anything to it. Just more small-town eccentricity. A crazy old woman and her equally flaky niece believing a tall tale like that. At least he didn't seem uncomfortable in her presence, although he had to know she'd overheard his dad's insensitive public announcement about the wedding. He certainly didn't need to worry that *she'd* make a reference to his situation, although she couldn't help but wonder what it was about him that had caused his bride-to-be to run.

Probably the cell phone.

"A lot of work ahead." He tapped the floor plan, dismissing the alleged hidden treasure and returning to the renovation.

She pointed. "You're taking out that wall?"

"Non-load-bearing, so it's okay." He winked. "The inn won't fall down."

"No, I mean, why do you want guests who are relaxing in the breakfast nook to look directly into the kitchen at the dirty dishes and stuff? People come to a place like this to get away from that kind of thing."

He studied the plan. "Well, it doesn't *have* to be taken out. I thought it would open up the space. Bring that garden light from the breakfast-nook windows into the kitchen."

She shook her head, reached for the mechanical pencil and drew the wall back in. She was going to have to watch this guy like a hawk. "And what's going on over here?"

"That's high shelving. Plants. Pottery."

"Who's going to get up there and keep them clean?"

Tight-lipped, Denny took the pencil from her, popped off the top cap to expose an eraser, then obliterated the shelving.

"I'm not trying to sabotage your plans. I'm trying to be practical." She tilted her head to read his extensive notes in the margin. "This doesn't have to all be done at once, does it?"

"Better to. On other renovation projects, I've found that one thing leads to another even though you initially think you might be able to do one at a time. Intending to redo the drywall reveals a wiring nightmare behind the scenes. A leak like the one in the parlor ceiling could point to a major plumbing overhaul."

"So everything's going to have to be ripped up? What about our guests?"

"Your primary summer season will be ending soon, won't it?"

"Aunt Viola says it winds down fairly rapidly after Labor Day." Not that they'd been fully booked the entire summer. "The Pinewood hasn't appealed much to the autumn and winter hunting crowd like Hunter's Hideaway does. But people in the hotter regions of the state still come up to hike and enjoy the autumn foliage. I'd have to check to see how many are booked."

"We'll need to make arrangements for them elsewhere. More expensive accommodations than the Pinewood, if necessary."

"There isn't a whole lot else in town. Just Hunter's Hideaway and another bed-and-breakfast or two."

"Then we may need to look farther afield. You mentioned a few neighboring towns. Canyon Springs. Show Low. And of course, from today onward, you and your aunt shouldn't reserve additional rooms until closer to Thanksgiving. Or better yet, until closer to Christmas. Steer them elsewhere."

That shouldn't be too hard to do. It wasn't like people were beating down the doors to get in. But it would still impact much-needed revenue.

"The scheduled garden events can continue as planned, correct? Teas and luncheons? They're catered by outside vendors who can park at the rear of the property and bring everything in through the back gate."

"That depends. You'll want to let them know what will be going on here. Power tools can be noisy."

Denny again bent over the floor plan to jot something down, and she couldn't help noticing his broad shoulders and muscled arms once more. Obviously his workouts included more than raising a cell phone to his ear.

He looked up at her. "Who's Barbie?"

Caught off guard, her brain scrambled to make sense of his question.

"How did you—? Oh, right. Aunt Vi mentioned her at lunch yesterday." He didn't need to know the whole scoop on Cameron's younger sister. "She's a local girl getting married in the garden the third weekend in October. A catered reception will follow there."

"Your aunt sounded as if renovations on the inn might be problematic for that. The wedding party booked rooms?"

"It would be wonderful if they had, but no." Lillian made a face of regret. "When I let Barbie look at them with that purpose in mind, from her reaction I was afraid she might cancel the wedding here altogether and go someplace else."

"So you're saying the timing of the work needs to keep the wedding in mind."

"Her family is prominent in the community and having everything torn up, giant waste containers sitting around, any kind of noise or distraction, definitely wouldn't go over with the bride or her family." Cameron's mother and grandmother would never forgive that. "You'll want to be especially careful of anything we're doing at the back of the house—window replacement and trim paint jobs— so things of that nature won't provide an unsightly background for wedding photographs."

"How bad would it affect the bottom line to encourage the bride to find another venue?"

Her eyes widened. She must have heard wrong. "You mean tell her she can't get married here?"

"I imagine there are other locations that would work equally well for her. You could—"

"No. Absolutely not."

He looked slightly taken aback. "Why?"

"She has her heart set on the garden. She got engaged at Christmas and has had it reserved since the first of the year."

No way was Lillian going to bring down further condemnation from her ex-fiancé's family on her aunt and herself. They had to live and do business in this town, and she had to regain her credibility after that runaway-bride fiasco left her a laughingstock. Considering Cameron's grandmother was on the library board, that episode could have already cost her a shot at the library manager position. Kicking Barbie out this close to her wedding day would be the last straw.

"I'm sorry, Denny, but having the wedding here is nonnegotiable."

"Third weekend in October, you said? Then that *will* be problematic."

"Sorry."

He tossed his pencil to the table, leveling his gaze at her. "And while we're discussing things that are potentially problematic…about that contractor we met at the Hideaway…"

"Todd. Todd Samuels." Her face warmed at the memory of yesterday's encounter. "Don't feel an obligation. He's a family friend who has a reputation for doing good work, but—"

"I have nothing against him, of course. But I'd like to check around. Get recommendations on others in the area who might be available, as well."

"Totally understandable." Personally, she'd rather not have Todd underfoot for weeks, her aunt plying him on a daily basis with her much-acclaimed pastries and pushing him at a niece who would hit the ripe old age of thirty before year's end.

While Aunt Viola may not have chosen to marry, she was a hopeless romantic when it came to the love lives of others. Always hoping and faithfully praying for happily-ever-afters on behalf of many a young lady and gent in the community.

Lillian included.

The ending to Lillian's former fiancé's sweep-her-off-her-feet courtship had been deeply disappointing—to both aunt and niece. But Lillian had learned her lesson, even if Aunt Viola hadn't.

Chapter Five

"Hey, Mister! You're here again."

Taylor opened the door to the inn when Denny arrived the next morning. The dining room was occupied, and she trailed behind him to the office where he spread out his sketches on the floor so he wouldn't have to clear the desk.

When she'd gotten home from school yesterday, Taylor had sat quietly at the end of the table watching him until her great-great-aunt called her for a late-afternoon snack. Cute kid, although not especially talkative. He'd tried to draw her out several times, but with little success. So she was Lillian's sister's child. What was her story, anyway?

From what Lillian said in relation to wanting to live in Hunter Ridge for her aunt's and niece's benefit as much as for her own, it sounded as if she thought the girl might remain with her for a while. But he sensed a mutual discomfort in interactions between aunt and niece.

He squatted and opened the big graph paper tablet to the first-floor draft. Taylor sat cross-legged beside him.

He'd told her yesterday what he was doing. Showed

her how he'd measured the rooms by letting her hold the
end of the tape measure while he demonstrated the technique, then explained how a foot—twelve inches—on
the measuring tape translated to the much smaller grid
on the paper.

"Aunt Viola says you're going to tear the house up
and put it back together again like those people on TV."

"That's the plan."

"I can help." Not a question. Not a request. A state-
ment. But what could he find for a kid to do that would
keep her out from underfoot? A renovation site held potential dangers for both kids and adults. "I can hit a wall
with a hammer. Or kick it down for you."

A demolition-day protégée in the making.

He smiled at her serious face. "I don't think we'll be
pulling down too many walls—" Lillian had nixed that
"—but I imagine we can find something you can do."

He'd have to give it some thought. Get Lillian's permission for whatever he came up with.

"Taylor! There you are." Lillian stood in the office
doorway, exasperation in her expression. "Tessa and her
mom are in the car waiting for you. You're going to make
everybody late for school."

The little girl shot her an aggrieved look, then scooted
closer to Denny. "I don't want to go to school today. I want
to stay here and help Mister tear things up."

"He's not tearing anything up," Lillian reassured her.

Taylor frowned, then looked up at him for confirmation.

"Your aunt is right. Not today."

Her little shoulders slumped. "Bummer."

"Let's get going, Taylor." Lillian held out her hand.
"You don't want to be late."

Taylor hesitated a long moment, a rebel spirit rising. But then abruptly she stood and patted his shoulder, her eyes boring into his. "Promise you won't tear anything up?"

"Promise."

She let out a sigh, then squeezed past Lillian, ignoring her aunt's outstretched hand.

"Don't forget your backpack, Taylor," she called after her, then turned a weary gaze on him. "She's usually more cooperative."

"You can fault me for that. She's intrigued with what I'm doing here. She wants to help, and I told her I'd find something for her to do. Hope that's okay."

"Kicking down walls?"

"How'd you guess?"

"I saw her practicing a kung-fu kick before she sat down for breakfast."

He chuckled. "I promise she won't be kicking down walls without *extreme* supervision. She's fascinated with the floor plans, and I predict you may have a future architect or contractor on your hands. I suspect by the time this is over, she and I will be great buddies."

"From how things looked this morning, I think you already are. I hope she wasn't being a nuisance."

"Not a chance, although I imagine we'll need to keep a close eye on her once work gets under way."

"Definitely."

He got to his feet. "If you don't mind my asking, is your sister ill? Is that why her daughter is living with you?"

"No illness. My little sister, as dear as she is and as much as I love her, isn't really into parenting. It's an inconvenience for her at best, and periodically she wearies of its restrictions and drops Taylor off with me for weeks. Often months."

"That has to be hard. Both for you and Taylor."

"It's heartrending each time my sister returns to claim her. And bewildering for Taylor when it happens again and again. I've watched her change over the years from a happy, laughing toddler to a more withdrawn, sometimes sullen youngster."

"Trust issues." He could relate to that. "You've had her in counseling, I suppose?"

She didn't take offense at his question. "Each time she's returned to me, we meet with a church or school counselor—of course, there's nothing like that on the other end when she's taken away again. Her mother visited for a few hours on Saturday, which is probably why we're seeing a lack of cooperation right now. That will ease, hopefully, by the weekend. But I know deep down she's confused and angry at her mother. Probably with me, too."

"I'm sorry Taylor—and you—are going through this. It may be especially difficult when she reaches adolescence."

He'd boiled over internally during those years, but with willpower he still didn't understand, he was able to rein in destructive feelings and focus on a single lifelong goal—earning the respect of everyone he met.

Lillian's hands fluttered almost helplessly. "I know God says not to, but I worry about that. Our folks weren't real hands-on parents, either, and Annalise tended to be a free spirit in need of more guidance than most. I don't want to see a repeat performance in this next generation."

"Is there a father in the picture?"

She shook her head. "Annalise was pretty wild and

got pregnant when she was sixteen. Insisted on keeping her baby, but refused to tell anyone who the father was. I suspect it wasn't about stubbornness, but because she didn't have a clue."

"Stormy start for a sweet kid like Taylor." He'd had a mother who mostly left him with sitters when he was small, and by the middle of grade school when twin baby sisters arrived, at a private school. He had a father and a stepfather, too, but neither had been much of a dad to him. Probably because, as he eventually grew to recognize, he wasn't that lovable. He'd learned to live with that reality, but he hated to see Taylor, who was plenty lovable, in that same spot. "I feel for her. I know what it's like to be set aside. To feel like you're in the way."

Lillian tilted her head slightly, a spark of curiosity in her eyes. Now, why had he gone and shared that, like some kind of crybaby?

"Taylor's blessed to have you and your aunt in her life." He gave her an assuring nod, certain of his words despite having known them but a few days. "You can rest easy, because I imagine that will make all the difference in the world."

"I hope and pray so. I wish there was a way…" Her words came wistfully. Then she took a sharp breath as her gaze again caught his. "Oh, I'm sorry. Too much information, for certain. You asked a simple question and I dumped everything on you. Please accept my apology."

"No, no, don't think of it like that. I genuinely like Taylor and I wanted to understand her situation." He offered a smile intended to set Lillian at ease. "In fact, I *needed* to know, since it looks like she and I may soon be a team. Who knows what this blossoming partnership could lead to? Perhaps a home-improvement reality TV show."

She laughed, which had been his intention.

"Promise you won't suggest it to her? She'll never let us hear the end of it until the cameras are rolling."

He held up his hand in a Boy Scout pledge. "I promise."

For a delightfully long moment their gazes held in shared amusement, an unfamiliar warmth curling around his heart. He hardly knew Lillian, yet he was talking to her like he'd never talked to Corrine. His former fiancée was about fashion, career climbing and who was who on the social roster.

Not kids. Family. God.

Nothing soul-deep or *too* personal.

That, in actuality, *should* have made them a perfect match. Had they taken one of those relationship compatibility tests, they'd have likely scored off the charts side by side. *So what went wrong?*

Realizing his intense gaze was making Lillian uncomfortable, he looked down at the floor plans. "So what do you say we get down to business? I want to call contractors today, so I need a handle on what we're agreeing to do here."

Despite his words, he hadn't given up the idea of bringing the GylesStyle team on board. But he'd do his best to at least give Lillian and her aunt the impression he wasn't taking their concerns about not using local craftsmen lightly.

"I do have a few decorating ideas. We didn't get around to discussing that direction yesterday. Let me run and get my tote bag. Be back in a minute."

She had interior-design ideas? That was something

generally left to a professional designer for GylesStyle properties, but he was going to have to wing this place on his own. Clearly what was needed here was a contemporary tailored look that would banish the gloom. Ironically, as much as he hadn't wanted anything to do with tossing good money after bad—still didn't, considering what might be transpiring back at the home office—he enjoyed envisioning what the finished product would look like.

He'd gotten his kicks out of that in the past, too, drawing satisfaction from the several times he'd served as the manager of one of those new-to-the-GylesStyle-fold properties. He liked seeing people enjoying something that had started as an idea in his head. Enjoyed making them feel special. At home. Thankfully, his stepfather ensured he had an appreciation of the world of hospitality from the ground up, sending him across the country on summer internships throughout high school and college.

He did need to talk to his mother about those vacant buildings on either side of the Pinewood, though, which detracted considerably from the image he wanted the upgraded inn to portray. Did she have any plans for them at all?

"Here we go." Lillian entered the room with an excited smile, and he immediately found himself smiling back. She pushed aside items on the desk, then slid out the contents of her tote bag and spread them across the polished surface. Notes. Article clippings. Magazine spreads.

His smile froze as he stared down at the colorful array of glossy magazine images and what appeared to be photocopies from books. Curvy-legged tables. Gilded mirrors. Poufy floral comforters with ruffled pastel bed skirts. China bric-a-brac. Enough crocheted and beribboned throw pillows to outfit an English country estate.

"My dream inn." Lillian made a sweeping motion to the desktop display, her eyes dancing with anticipation of his response. "What do you think?"

"I... Wow. Colorful. Feminine."

Denny gazed down at the desk as if held rapt by the beautiful display, and a tingle of excitement raced through Lillian as she awaited his approval.

"And I see," he added, "that you're fond of florals."

"I thought it would be perfect to carry over from the garden, don't you think? Unify the theme, since it's the garden that draws guests here." She picked up a photo of a canopied four-poster bed. "I was wondering...should the inn be renamed? Would that be hard to do? I was thinking maybe the Secret Garden Inn. Or Pinegarden Inn, if we wanted it to sound more mountain country-ish."

"I hadn't given any thought to renaming. You're ahead of me there."

Dreaming up names and ideas had been a diversion when she first came to Hunter Ridge and the librarian job, managing the inn and taking care of her aunt got too overwhelming.

"Sorry. I've been giving this a lot of thought since I first came here to help Aunt Viola. I let my imagination run wild for when the place could be redecorated."

"I can see that." He motioned to the images. "What does your aunt think of your ideas?"

"She loves them. I was afraid she might be unwilling to go light and bright after living here so long in the shadows, but she's on board. Excited about it."

At long last, this is going to happen. Our dreams for the inn will finally come true.

Denny continued to gaze down at her array of clippings. Moved a few around. But he wasn't smiling now. In fact, it was slowly dawning on her that he'd avoided looking at her since she'd spread out the fruits of her imaginings on the desk.

"Is this," she said in a more subdued tone, "similar to what you're envisioning?"

Pursing his lips, he propped his hands on his hips and continued to stare down at the desk. "Not exactly."

Oh. She hadn't thought about the fact that he might have ideas beyond what needed to happen structurally— the electrical and plumbing, insulation, and the kick-down-the-wall stuff. Regarding the decorating, she'd thought that at most his mother might have a few suggestions she would gladly incorporate.

Lillian studied him, willing him to look at her. "So… how far off the mark are we from each other?"

The look he delivered when his gaze finally met hers was bleak. "From here to Mars and back. I'm sorry, Lillian. I can see you spent a lot of time and thought on this but—"

"But what?" She swallowed, fighting back disappointment.

"It's too much."

"How so?"

"I thought I heard voices in here," Aunt Viola commented cheerfully from the doorway.

But she wasn't drawn to the desk and its scattered photos, which clued in Lillian that her hip might be giving her problems this morning, and she feared Denny might pick up on it. She'd been relying on a walker or cane in the apartment or elsewhere, but managed to avoid using them when Charlotte's son was around.

"Making decorating decisions, are you?" Aunt Vi nodded her approval. "Can't you imagine cuddling on a cool evening under one of those big cozy comforters?"

"Denny doesn't care for my ideas," Lillian said flatly before her aunt got too enthusiastic.

Aunt Viola gave him a disbelieving frown. "What's not to like?"

If a man could ever be said to squirm, Denny was doing just that right now under her aunt's laser-like glare. "It's not...suitable."

"What's that supposed to mean?"

"It's not in keeping with the vibe we need here." His words were spoken carefully. "And as lovely as they are, the delicate bed linens and other fabric elements won't stand up to the frequency of launderings required in a commercial establishment."

"Wash them on delicate."

He smiled indulgently. "A proliferation of knickknacks and furnishings with curlicues carved into them will only serve as dust collectors. There's a reason why old estates were overrun with house servants." He gave Lillian an apologetic look. "And while I'm not entirely opposed to a feminine touch, let's remember men should feel equally comfortable."

Aunt Viola rolled her eyes. "So tie a ribbon around a horseshoe, hang it over the door and be done with it."

Lillian cringed. This was not going how she had envisioned the "reveal" of her decorating ideas. While irritated that Denny had rejected her vision—which she still thought was a good one—she could see his point as far as maintenance. But for the most part, it was women who made the reservations at a bed-and-breakfast. Often for a girlfriends' weekend, a sister weekend, or a mother-daughter or grandmother-mother-daughter retreat. Surely it wouldn't kill a man to occasionally indulge his sweetheart in a fabulously romantic overnight stay?

Which told her exactly where romance rated in Denny Hunter's book. That might explain a lot about why his lady had bolted at the last minute.

But Aunt Vi wasn't done with him yet.

"Young man, don't you think you should run Lillian's ideas by your mother? She owns this place, in case you've forgotten."

"I haven't forgotten, ma'am," he said quietly, and Lillian actually felt sorry for him. Having headed up the local library for decades, her aunt had mastered the put-you-in-your-place persona when needed. No doubt he felt as if he were ten years old and being shushed for whispering among the book stacks.

"Good. Then that's taken care of." She turned to Lillian. "Barbie called again. She'd like you to call her back."

"What's it about this time?" And why didn't Barbie use Lillian's cell number as requested instead of calling the inn's number and getting Aunt Viola involved? Her aunt found dealing with the bride-to-be stressful.

"Something she doesn't like about the caterer."

"The bride contracts directly with them, and our part is only cooperating with the vendor to make certain he or she has everything needed from our end."

"I know, I know. But you know Barbie."

Yes, she did. All too well. This event was certainly not one she looked forward to, especially considering it was likely Cameron Gray would fly in from Boston for his sister's nuptials.

When Aunt Viola left the room, Lillian turned to Denny, who was again studying the remnants of her fledgling design dreams.

"May I see your concept, Denny? Or do you not have anything worked up yet?"

"I have something in draft form." He retrieved the graph paper pad from the floor and placed it on the desk, then flipped to the back, where he'd sketched out several renderings in colored felt-tip marker.

She couldn't help but laugh as she took in the bold strokes. Bare spaces. Clean-lined furnishings in what appeared to be leather, glass—and *chrome*? No way.

"No offense, Denny, but you think *this* is in keeping with the vibe we need here? With a building set in ponderosa-pine mountain country that's closing in on a hundred years old? With a clientele that's predominantly female, no less?"

His concept was far more modern and masculine than she'd have ever dreamed up in a thousand years. Surprisingly, though, he had an artist's eye for perspective, texture and color. But that didn't make up for the chrome.

"Something similar—to a more upscale degree—has been extremely popular in another GylesStyle Inn in Aspen, Colorado. Big-time mountain country."

She could concede something simpler than her ideas might be a better route to go. But stark? Downright austere? She'd hate staying in a place like that. It would be like trying to relax in a showroom window display.

This was going to be a long month and a half.

"Well, don't you think Aspenites are a different animal than those of more modest means who are drawn to rustic Hunter Ridge? You're not intending to incorporate the Pinewood into the GylesStyle family of inns, are you?"

"That's not the intention. This is solely a pet project of my mother's. But she has the money and will want to do it right."

"Then I suggest something less, shall we say, streamlined? Urban? I'm aware of minimalism's popularity these days. But no doubt you're aware that Hunter's Hideaway falls into the rustic style of things, and they pretty much stay booked year-round. People still gravitate to a more traditional, homey type of place to kick back in. Sure, they shop at health-food stores and cling to their Wi-Fi connections, but they haven't abandoned a secret indulgence in comfort food or a hunger for more down-to-earth accommodations."

"The Hideaway *is* doing well," he admitted. "And will do even better once it fully launches its plan to promote itself as a destination spot for reunions, anniversary celebrations and the like. It's a perfect complement to the hunters, hikers and horsemen who have been its traditional target audience. I wouldn't have a spot there right now except a cabin needed repairs done before it could be reserved by guests, and Uncle Dave agreed to put that off and rent it to me since I'm family."

"See?"

"What I can't see is the Pinewood Inn decked out with Navajo-blanketed bunk beds, deer heads on the wall and cattle brands burned into the woodwork."

He wasn't even *trying* to understand what she was saying, and she didn't have time to talk sense into him. She had to get to work for a meeting.

She reached for the tote bag, intending to gather the remains of her rejected proposal.

Denny held up his hand. "Leave that, please. I'd like to look through what you have here."

She shook her head. "Don't humor me. I'm a big girl."

"I'm not humoring you. I want to take a closer look. See if there's anything here that can be incorporated into my own ideas. I'm sorry if I hurt you. That wasn't my intention."

"You didn't hurt me." Okay, maybe a little. "I'm disappointed, I guess. But you're the pro, not me."

"You told me, though, that you've stayed in a lot of hospitality properties. That you know what others like and don't like. What *you* like and don't like. I'd be remiss if I didn't take a potential paying guest's viewpoint into consideration, now wouldn't I?"

She felt as if she were being given a pat on the head and sent on her way. But at least he wasn't antagonistic or hostile about their differing opinions. Which was more than she could say for Aunt Viola when she had leaped in to straighten him out.

"I'm sorry my aunt lit into you."

"No problem. She's right. Anything I do will be approved first by my mother. I'm not used to working like this, with someone directing over my shoulder, but this project holds a special place in my mother's heart. As it does in your aunt's. Let me see what I can come up with by way of a compromise."

With a forced smile, she gave a brisk nod, then headed out the door.

Compromise.

English cottage and minimalist chrome?

She wasn't holding her breath on that one.

Chapter Six

By the end of the day Friday, Denny had come to a dis-
heartening conclusion.

His customary GylesStyle contractor in this region
couldn't squeeze in a rush project at the inn before his
next one was scheduled, due to being out for rotator-cuff
surgery. And his backup's wife was having a C-section,
so that guy was taking time off, too. Even regionally, no
one else who received adequately positive endorsements
was available.

Which left Viola's top pick. Todd Samuels.

Oh well.

Gratefully donning a change of clothes from the big
box he'd sweet-talked one of his Gyles half sisters into
overnighting, he was intent on getting to town and catching Lillian before she left work to pick up Taylor from a
friend's house. He'd just exited the cabin when his dad
hailed him from a couple of cabins over, where he must
have been visiting someone.

He reached the Porsche just as Denny did. "Where
have you been keeping yourself?"

"Getting that Pinewood Inn project I told you about up and running."

"I can't believe your mother's pigheadedly hanging on to that property. And the two next door. How long have those sat vacant? But no, she refuses to sell them back to me, or to anyone else, for that matter. Now that's cutting off your nose to spite your face, if you ask me." He wagged his finger. "Remember that, son. Don't go getting yourself hitched to some female whose middle name is Stubborn."

"No danger of that in the immediate future."

"Still pining after that minx who dumped you? Good riddance, I say!"

Denny was increasingly coming to that same conclusion, although he had to concede that snagging his stepbrother put Corrine in a more socially prominent position than a lowly stepson of Elden Gyles would ever have attained for her. He should probably send Vic a thank-you note for sparing him what would probably have been a rocky marriage.

Dad nodded to the Porsche. "You must be doing all right if you're driving one of these."

"It was a surprise birthday present from Mother on my thirtieth. Delivered right to my door."

"Your mom gave you that? La-di-da. Don't go looking at me on your fortieth. You're on your own. I'm surprised Char knew enough about cars to pick this one out."

"Elden did."

Dad waved him away. "Don't go talkin' to me about Elden. I had to listen to Elden this and Elden that when I was first dating your mother. They'd broken up, and fool that I was, I let her sob on my shoulder between classes at the university."

"I'm not getting in the middle of that, Dad. But we both know she wasn't happy living in Hunter Ridge."

"Of course she wasn't. Not with that rich hotel mogul still calling her. Sending flowers. Whining about how he'd made the biggest mistake of his life in breaking up with her."

"Why did they break up?" Denny knew she and Elden had met when she was doing an internship at GylesStyle Inns between her junior and senior years as part of her marketing degree. His mother never talked about the breakup, and he'd never thought to ask.

"His father didn't think she was good enough for his baby boy." Dad sneered. "She didn't have a suitable pedigree or run in the right hoity-toity crowd. Ironic, huh? Her folks didn't think *I* was good enough for *her*."

Denny glanced at his watch. "Sorry, Dad, but I have to run. I'm meeting with—with a business colleague. I don't want to be late."

The faster he got Lillian's approval of the interior sketches, the more quickly he could run them by his mother and leave the rest in the hands of a contractor. No way was he going to personally babysit the Pinewood's upgrade. Once he got the ball rolling, he'd be out of here.

While he had to lie low away from the main office, that didn't mean he had to hide out in Hunter Ridge. There were GylesStyle properties across the country that he had the responsibility of overseeing. Plenty to keep him busy and out of Vic's way.

"Yeah, go on, city boy, if you're in such a big hurry that you don't have time to shoot the breeze with your old man. Get out of here." His dad stalked off.

Denny was tempted to catch up with him, assure him that time spent together while he was in town was important to him. Then he decided against it. Giving his father an opportunity to further rant about his ex-wife and her husband did neither of them any favors.

In town, Denny parked in front of the stone library off the main road, then trotted up the stairs and eased open the heavy door. The hush and the scent of books sent him reeling back to the library he'd loved as a kid when, at age nine, he'd been shipped off to a private school back East. The hundred-and-fifty-year-old book-filled space had become his home away from home. The one place he might be alone but never felt lonely. He'd forgotten about that and hadn't set foot in a library since his university days.

No one was at the front desk. Had he missed her?

It didn't take long to cruise through the tall stacks—despite pausing here and there to scan the titles—before finally finding her in an office at the back.

"Hey, Lillian."

She turned, her surprise evident at finding he'd invaded her territory. She smiled, then glanced at the older woman seated behind a desk. "Jeri, this is Denny Hunter. Denny, Jeri Saldana, our library manager since Aunt Vi retired. Denny's mother owns the Pinewood Inn, and he's here to see about fixing it up."

They exchanged pleasantries, and then Denny nodded to the purse clutched in Lillian's hands. "Do you have a quick minute before you leave? I won't keep you long. I know you said earlier that you had to get Taylor someplace."

"To the church. There's a rehearsal for the grade-schoolers' presentation on Sunday morning. A Labor Day theme."

"This will just take a few minutes."

Walking her to the door and out on the front steps, he

scrolled through the photos on his phone until he found the ones he'd taken of his latest renderings of the inn. "I want you to take a look at these. Give me your honest feedback before I forward them to my mother tonight."

It had been eating at him that he'd wounded Lillian's feelings when he'd bluntly rejected her ideas. Although she denied it, he hadn't missed the flash of hurt in her eyes.

She slipped her purse strap over her shoulder and took the phone from him, her fingers gently brushing his. Then her eyes widened as she scrolled through the photos. He'd worked until midnight, his original concept taking on a softer, less bold and masculine feel. The simplicity of line was retained, but lighter tones of nature set off occasional pops of florals—a footstool, tailored throw pillows, boxed window toppers, a framed painting. Gone was the chrome, replaced by oak.

"What do you think?"

"I absolutely love this. You've taken the best of both our ideas and combined them in a way I'd never have thought could be done. Each guest room has a unique charm, so comfortable-looking. You are *amazing*, Denny Hunter."

"I like to think so."

She stared at him openmouthed. Then he laughed.

"Just kidding. So you like the concept now?"

"Oh, yes. Aunt Viola will be pleased we were able to come to a consensus—thanks to you."

"It wasn't all my doing. I merely drove the felt tips."

She made a cute face. "I *was* way off the mark with my ideas, wasn't I?"

"Not so far off."

She tipped her head to look at him doubtfully over the

top of her glasses. "What part of overabundance of pastels and reeking with florals did you overlook?"

He grinned. "Maybe you did get a tad carried away. But I took it to the other extreme."

Squinting one eye, she held up her hand, her thumb and forefinger about a half inch apart. "Maybe a tad."

"Agreed."

With a laugh, she pointed to the screen. "Look there, over the bedroom door—a horseshoe with a ribbon on it."

"I hoped you'd notice that."

"Aunt Vi will get such a kick out of it." With a last lingering look, she handed him his phone. "I'm awed at how you melded our diverse ideas into something extraordinary."

"Then with your blessing, off they go for my mother's seal of approval so we can get moving full speed ahead."

Feeling pretty proud of himself at the moment—that he'd smoothed the sharp edges off their last meeting—he'd just put away his phone when he sensed Lillian tense. Turning, he followed the trajectory of her gaze. Across the street a teenage boy, hands tucked under his armpits, was bobbing along like a regal potentate of poultry.

Chicken Man. Again.

"What is *wrong* with that kid?"

Lillian grasped his arm, turning him toward her. "He thinks he's funny and is trying to get attention."

Frowning, he glanced back again.

Her grip tightened. "If you don't pay him any mind, he'll move on. Don't give him the satisfaction of knowing he annoys you."

With effort, he managed to keep his back turned to the little twerp. "Can't he find anything better to do? Or is that a prime example of what happens to you when you live in a tiny town too long?"

Or maybe, like him, the kid didn't sleep well, and it had made him loopy. For the fourth night in a row, Denny had lain awake for hours. It was way too quiet around here at night—he didn't hear so much as a single cricket. Or maybe that sleeplessness had more to do with being unable to keep his thoughts off the lovely Lillian? What was wrong with him, anyway? She wasn't his type at all.

"It has nothing to do with small towns," Lillian said, "and everything to do with wanting to make a nuisance of himself."

"He's nailed that one."

Denny joined her as she headed down the steps and walked her to her car, a Honda CR-V. "Before you head out, you might like to know your aunt won."

Her brow crinkled. "Won what?"

"Her pick of contractors. I'm going with Todd Samuels."

He wasn't sure how to read her expression, but the tinge of pink in her cheeks said more than he wanted to know. Had she dated the guy in the past? Wanted to date him now?

She unlocked the car, and he opened the driver's-side door for her.

"He'll do good work for you, Denny."

"Keep your fingers crossed that he hasn't picked up another job since we talked to him on Tuesday. If he has, I'm up a creek without a contractor."

And chained to Hunter Ridge.

"Knowing Todd, he'll figure something out even if he has to burn the midnight oil to juggle two jobs at once.

He isn't afraid of hard work. You'll get your money's worth out of him."

And a front-row seat to a flirtation he'd prefer not to witness.

She slipped into the seat behind the steering wheel. "So where are you off to now?"

"I'll call Todd first. Then probably go back to the Hideaway. They're getting ready for that Labor Day charity barbecue Taylor sold me a ticket to. The place is humming with preparations, and I feel like I should be helping out, not standing around on the sidelines. That is, if they'll have me."

"Of course they'll have you, silly. You're a Hunter."

"A *long-lost* Hunter."

"Once a Hunter, always a Hunter, I imagine. You're part of an amazing family, Denny. Everyone—or most everyone—around here admires them. God-fearing, hardworking, family-comes-first folks."

"My mother never fit in with them. Doubtful I ever will, either."

Her expression softened. "You said earlier this week in connection to Taylor's situation that you know what it's like to feel set aside. To feel like you're in the way. Is that coming from the Gyles side or the Hunter side? Or both?"

He should have kept his mouth shut.

"It's that I was pulled out of Hunter Ridge when I was two, so no relationships built there." Dad, having started a second family with Vickie within two years of the divorce, hadn't made that much effort to reach out to him, probably thinking his ex-wife and her new husband had the parenting bases covered. "My stepfather already had a son and two daughters. So Elden Gyles had found his golden boy in my stepbrother, Vic, well before I came along."

Denny hoped that didn't come out sounding as bitter as he thought it might have. But he'd made his mark through hard work and unflagging loyalty. Earned the respect of those around him—including, he'd believed, his stepfather. Which was what made Vic's promotion such a blow.

Determined to get the conversation off himself, Denny cleared his throat before Lillian could respond. "You said something, didn't you, about your own parents not being real hands-on?"

He remembered that? So she must have said it aloud at some point. She'd found him surprisingly easy to talk to, and had likely let down her guard too quickly.

"They're both motivational speakers. They write articles and books and conduct workshops across the country and around the world." Kind of ironic that they'd made good money and received acclaim for telling other people how to get their acts together, yet their own daughters hungered for more attention than the allotted fifteen minutes a day of "quality time."

"No wonder you moved around a lot. GylesStyle Inns sometimes brings in motivational speakers—would I recognize their names?"

"Probably. Ilsa and Archer Keene."

His eyes widened. "Whoa."

Obviously his mind was trying to put two and two together, attempting to figure out how with "celebrity" parents, she'd ended up a part-time librarian in what he considered Podunk, Arizona.

"Yep, that's the scoop. But I've got to run. Taylor's been faithfully practicing her piece for the program this week, and I don't want her to miss the rehearsal."

"Then I'll talk to you later."

He shut her door, but she immediately turned the key in the ignition and rolled down the window.

"Will you be at church on Sunday? I know she'd love for her favorite demolition partner to see her recite. They have a song, too."

"Um…"

"You don't have to. I just thought—"

Thought what? As engaging as he was, she had no business setting up situations where she'd have to spend more time than necessary with Denny Hunter. Like Cameron, he was city through and through, and didn't try to hide his ridicule of Hunter Ridge like her former fiancé had done. Besides, the more he interacted with townspeople, the more likely he'd hear about her bye-bye bride episode. Which might leave him less inclined to cooperate with the renovation.

"Thanks for the invitation. Let's see how it goes, okay? You know, after I find out how I can help at the Hideaway for the charity barbecue. I imagine Saturday and Sunday will be all hands on deck for a big deal like that on Monday."

Knowing the Hunters, they'd be up at the crack of dawn and working until well after dark—but filling the pews for a time of worship when the church doors opened.

"Will you be coming by the inn tomorrow?"

"Doubtful."

"Then I'll see you on Monday when you make good use of that barbecue ticket."

With a wave, she backed out, noting thankfully that sometime during the conversation, Randy Gray had vanished.

How long was Cameron's brother going to keep up with the mockery? Surely he'd tire of it. He was fourteen, and wouldn't he be taking a serious interest in girls pretty soon? Who'd want to date a guy who clucked?

Once at the church, having picked up Taylor on the way, she dropped her off in a Sunday-school room serving as a staging area. Settling into a polished pew near the front of the auditorium, Lillian mulled over her last encounter with Denny.

To say that she'd been surprised when he showed up at the library would be an understatement. She also couldn't believe how he'd taken the time to bring both of their ideas for the interior together in such a winning combination. He was a much more agreeable—and kind— man than her impressions the first day or two had led her to believe. He could have insisted on his own ideas and let that be that.

She hadn't been at the church long when Pastor Garrett McCrae slipped into the seat beside her.

If only she and Cameron had taken premarital counseling from Garrett instead of asking her fiancé's college buddy—now a minister—to fly in and officiate a wedding in the pines. Surely they'd both have had their eyes opened and gotten their heads out of the clouds well before that disastrous day.

"When I saw Taylor after Sunday school last weekend, she told me Annalise had dropped by on Saturday." He kept his voice low. "How'd that go?"

"Like always."

"Hard."

She nodded. "I love my sister, but sometimes…"

"You want to strangle her."

That was what she loved about Garrett, and what made him a good pastor to his flock. He was so *real*. "I do."

"You'd mentioned a while back that you were thinking about taking legal action on Taylor's behalf to see if you could get custody."

"I'm not exactly in an ideal situation to pursue that. Single. Part-time job. Mooching housing from an elderly aunt. And that farce with Cameron left me looking like the town buffoon."

"Come on now."

"That's what the lawyer I talked to said. And he's right. On the surface, what do I have to offer that's better than what Taylor's mother provides? We both keep her periodically, not full-time. Neither of us owns the roof over our head. At least Annalise provides a male role model a good deal of the time, which is more than I can claim."

Garrett leaned forward, his steady gray eyes intent. "Lillian, if you think those men who come and go in your sister's life are role models, we need to have a long talk."

She made a face. "Oh, I know. I'm just torn right now. Taylor is obviously unhappy. She's not developing friendships, despite my making an effort to get her to playdates and special events where she can get to know kids her age. Like this rehearsal."

Lillian nodded to the front of the church, where the children had filed out to await further direction. "Look at her, Garrett. Standing off to the side, waiting her turn to recite, but not engaged. Not really present. I think she's afraid to connect with people, knowing how badly it's going to hurt when her mom uproots her again."

"You moved around a lot as a kid, too, and didn't put down much in the way of roots, either."

She'd never been a wild child, though, like Annalise. Or Garrett. She could still vaguely remember the days when he sported a ponytail and a questionable reputation.

"But I had Aunt Viola. And my books. And God. Although I didn't get to come here as often as I'd have liked, I did sink my roots down in Hunter Ridge. Annalise hated to read and didn't like coming to Aunt Vi's, where she'd have to behave herself. She despised anything having to do with God. Saw Him as the big spoilsport in the sky."

Garrett nodded silently, and she knew he was praying somewhere down deep inside. He wasn't one to offer quick fixes and platitudes.

"Garrett!" someone called from the platform. "You're up next."

He stood, placing his hand lightly on her shoulder. "This will work out, Lillian. I don't know when or how, but I do know God loves you and Taylor. And Annalise, too."

He'd just reached the podium when, to Lillian's shock, a smile spread across Taylor's face, and she started excitedly hopping up and down as she looked to the back of the church.

Lillian swiftly turned to glimpse Denny coming down the side aisle. He lifted a hand in greeting to her niece, the index finger of his other hand pressed to his lips in a shushing motion. Looking chagrined at drawing attention to himself, he slipped into the spot Garrett had vacated.

"I didn't expect to see you here," she whispered.

"I thought since I probably won't attend Sunday, coming to the rehearsal might make it up to Taylor."

"Look at her. What do you think?"

Up front, her niece had grown still, but a smile beamed across the vast space in Denny's direction. He grinned back at her, and it seemed it was all Taylor could do to focus on the woman who was lining them up on the portable risers.

"I think I made her day."

"You think? You made her week. Maybe the entire month."

They gave their full attention to the proceedings, Taylor focusing solely on Denny when she recited her piece with more gusto than she'd ever exhibited while practicing at home.

But while it was thrilling to see her niece so exuberant, reminiscent of her toddler years, warning bells went off in Lillian's head. Taylor had connected with Denny. Not Garrett. Not the father of one of her schoolmates. Why? As much as she'd originally have been glad to be rid of him, Denny wouldn't be around long. How would that impact Taylor?

When the children were dismissed, her niece came charging down the aisle, straight for Denny. "Mister!"

For a moment Lillian thought she'd fling herself into his arms, but she abruptly halted in front of him and stood there uncertainly, looking from Denny to her and back again.

"You came," she said quietly, considerably more subdued. But happiness filled her eyes. "I didn't know you were coming. You didn't tell me."

He patted her arm. "I didn't know myself. It's a surprise for us both."

She giggled. "Was it a surprise for you, too, Aunt Lillian?"

"A *big* surprise." She had no idea Denny would have such a soft heart for the little girl.

As they headed for the exit, she looked down at Taylor. "Where's your sweater?"

She shrugged. "In the Sunday-school room?"

"I'll get it. You stay with Denny. I'll meet you both outside."

Navigating the maze of hallways, Lillian was nearing a corner when she heard her name spoken in a hushed female tone. Instinctively she halted, out of sight.

"Can you believe it? She's caught herself another one. And a mighty fine-looking one, although Cameron was plenty nice to look at, as well."

"I saw them standing together outside the library earlier. Heard she wants to snag Jeri's spot when she retires. I hope the library advisory board looks long and hard at *that* application."

"You know they will. Cameron's grandmother is on the board."

"I wonder if Lillian will throw this latest catch back, too?"

A snicker.

"You'd think a gal who comes to church regularly and claims to know God wouldn't be so fickle. Poor Viola."

"Viola? Poor new boyfriend, in my book. Who *is* he, anyway?"

Barely able to breathe, Lillian strained to hear. But the voices faded as the women headed in the opposite direction to the fellowship hall.

She pressed shaking hands to her mouth.

They're laughing at me. Making fun of me. Doubting my suitability for the librarian position.

Momentarily frozen in her tracks, every fiber of her being nevertheless wanted to run. Run as far as her legs would carry her from Hunter Ridge and gossiping tongues. She hadn't recognized the voices in the whispery exchange. But maybe that was for the best. Could she ever face them, knowing how they felt about her? Judged her? Mocked her?

Deep breath.

She lowered her hands, willing them to stop shaking and her heart rate to slow down.

This, too, shall pass. This, too, shall pass.

Denny and Taylor would be wondering what happened to her. Forcing herself to move forward, she quickly retrieved Taylor's sweater from a nearby classroom. Then on unsteady legs, she hurried back to the auditorium and out the front door to where Denny and Taylor awaited her.

The little girl's hand was clasped in his.

Were people noticing? Wondering? Assuming, like the two gossipmongers, that Denny was the latest man in her life? And that he was walking down the gangplank, unaware the runaway bride was about to shove him off?

"Here's your sweater." She handed it to Taylor, who released Denny's hand to take it. "Ready to go?"

"Mister wants to take us out to eat." Her niece looked up at him with open affection.

Wonderful. No way was she going to be seen around town with Denny Hunter after that encounter outside the Sunday-school rooms. She had a reputation to preserve, and people reviving something that had happened months ago didn't bode well for her job prospects.

She returned Denny's uncertain smile. "Thanks for the invitation. That's sweet of you. But it's been a long week, and I think I'd better get Taylor home, fix a light supper and get her to bed at a decent hour."

"But Mister wants—"

"Taylor." Lillian gave her "the look." Her niece frowned but ceased to whine.

Denny walked them to her car, and with every single step she was aware of those still lingering in the parking lot after the rehearsal. Felt all the eyes on her and the handsome Hunter.

It was considerate of him to invite them to dinner. It *had* been a long, stressful week—mostly due to Denny's unexpected arrival—and it would be nice not to have to go home and fix a meal. But she wasn't about to risk being seen with him.

When she got Taylor situated in the back seat, she turned to Denny. "Thanks again for coming tonight. You made a little girl very, very happy."

"And her genuine delight made a big boy very, very happy. She's a great kid."

"She is."

"If you could do me a favor, though…" He lowered his voice. "Please don't let her get her hopes up that I'll be there for her Sunday service program, too. I wouldn't want her to be disappointed."

"I'll make sure she understands."

"Thanks."

"And thank you again for offering to take us out to eat. It's that, you know…tonight's not… It won't work out."

"I understand." He stepped away and waved to Taylor. "See you both later."

Lillian had driven but a block when she looked in the rearview mirror at her niece. "What do you say we surprise Aunt Viola by picking up pizza for supper?"

Both Aunt Vi and Taylor loved pizza.

But no cheer came from the back seat.

Chapter Seven

"Get over it, Hunter," Denny mumbled under his breath three days later as he reflected again on the last time he'd seen Taylor and Lillian.

He'd almost fallen over when Taylor announced that he wanted to take her and Lillian out to eat. Where had that come from? Not out of *his* mouth. As she'd looked up at him with such hope in her eyes, though, he'd quickly concluded it was a pretty good idea after all. But before he could get the words out, Lillian made sure he clearly understood it wasn't such a hot suggestion.

It wasn't like he was asking Lillian out on a date or something. In fact, *he* hadn't asked her and Taylor out at all. But the sting of rejection irritated, like a scratchy T-shirt.

"Den! We could use your help over here."

"Sure 'nuff." He abandoned the table umbrellas he'd been setting up on the huge patio in back of the Inn at Hunter's Hideaway and headed to where cousins Luke and Grady and some dude named Sawyer Banks, who ran an outdoor gear shop, were wrangling the setup of a sound stage. A regional country-and-western band was scheduled to start belting out songs from there that afternoon and into the evening.

He'd never been one for that kind of music. Give him a full symphony orchestra or easy jazz any day. But with speakers thumping out country hits since he'd first joined the laboring Hunters on Saturday morning, he could admit it might be growing on him. And the scent of barbecued beef and pork sizzling in the huge barrel grills today sealed the deal. No offense, Beethoven.

"You've come in pretty handy the past few days," Luke commented as they pounded the sound-stage flooring into place and stepped back to admire their handiwork. "I have to admit I'm kind of surprised a city slicker who drives a Porsche knows so much about tearing things apart and putting them back together."

Luke, a big guy about six or seven years Denny's senior and now a father of four, had been in the armed services when Denny visited here the last time as a twelve-year-old. So he didn't have memories of Luke. Now Grady and Garrett, those two were a different matter. Back then, the three of them had gotten off on the wrong foot from the word go. Thankfully, Grady had mellowed considerably in the intervening years and gotten himself married. Old animosities might not yet be swept under the rug, but nobody was trying to punch out anybody's lights by this point.

Not that Denny thought Charlotte Gyles had been forgiven for her perceived wrongdoing. Luke had earlier openly addressed the hard feelings she'd left behind when she'd walked out on his uncle Doug, dragged Denny off with her and snatched Hunter properties with the help of her high-powered lawyers. Denny got the distinct impression that as her son—being half Hunter—he'd be tolerated only as long as he minded his p's and q's. It was like being on probation of sorts.

"I've spent a lot of years behind the hotel industry scenes," he reminded his cousin. "Scouting structures and envisioning them repurposed. I find great pleasure in taking something that isn't working as well as it could and giving it a brand-new life."

Grady laughed. "Kind of a God-like perspective, isn't it?"

"I suppose so." He'd never thought of it that way. Not that he was opposed to God or anything.

"Hey, kids!" Uncle Dave, his dad's older brother, stood at the back entrance to the inn. Denny would have given just about anything to have had a dad like him. "When you finish up here, get back to the table setup so the gals have time to fancy them up before our guests start arriving."

"Why are the *gals* always responsible for making things pretty?" A spunky blonde appeared at her dad's side, her hands on her hips in a show of defiance. It was Denny's cousin Rio, who'd been about a year old when he'd last visited. A top-notch handler of horses, she was in college now and engaged to a cowboy who worked with the horse operation at the Hideaway. She and Cash Herrera would be wed in December.

"Because, Rio," big brother Luke drawled, "you'll wait into next year if you think one of us can top you and the other ladies in that department. Although—" he cut a look in Denny's direction "—*this* one can draw pretty pictures if you need some."

The other men laughed. So much for getting any respect for the photographed sketches of the inn he'd shared yesterday. Speaking of which, he still hadn't heard anything from his mother, either positive or negative. Maybe she and Elden had taken off for a three-day weekend, although he didn't know how far his mother was supposed to get from rehab.

When they'd finished table setup and the ladies moved in to take over, he headed back to the cabin shortly after noon to get cleaned up. His cousins took no prisoners when it came to their sense of humor at his expense—as his brief riding lesson yesterday afternoon would attest.

Nor could he say he felt at ease among them. He was getting the impression they were keeping an eye on his every move. But oddly, their ribbing felt good. There had never been much in the way of camaraderie in the Gyles household. No bonding.

A brother of the heart would never have done to Denny what Vic had done to him.

Back at the sprawling, pine-shaded patio, now dotted with open-umbrella tables and fresh flowers, the band was tuning up and a sizable crowd had already gathered. It had been a few years since the Hunter clan had hosted one of these charity deals, so excitement ran high. Apparently a Hunter-hosted bash was historically known to top them all.

Overhead, dark clouds gathered, and there was some grumbling that a stray monsoon thundershower might be in store. But he got the impression that rain for the surrounding forest would nevertheless be welcomed. It was gorgeous country that his Hunter side of the family called home, and its peaceful beauty began to seep down inside him.

"Mister!"

Already smiling before he turned in Taylor's direction, he couldn't help but feel more wanted by her than either of his families made him feel. There was something about being greeted like a long-lost friend by a sweet kid that assured him he had a right to be alive. That he belonged.

"Howdy there, little missy." Ugh. He was starting to sound like a country boy. Too many golden-oldie country-and-western hits.

Taylor trotted up to him. "Did you bring your ticket?"

He felt around in his pocket, then produced it. It was battered, but in one piece. "Right here."

"Lemme see your number. You can win a prize."

"That's what I heard."

"You're 1566." After studying it intently, she handed the ticket back to him, then turned and called into the crowd, "Aunt Lillian, Mister remembered his ticket."

Seated at a nearby table with her back to them, Lillian rose somewhat reluctantly. She probably still thought he'd been asking her out a few nights ago and didn't want to encourage his attention. Like he'd be inclined to get involved with a small-town librarian? Nope. No, thanks.

"Denny does have a name, Taylor." She cast him an apologetic look as she joined them.

He smiled, noticing how she'd swept her hair up, tiny silver hoop earrings peeping out from beneath a few stray strands of dark hair. "Mister works fine, too."

Taylor tugged on his sleeve. "You stay here with Aunt Lillian so she doesn't get lost. I have to help Aunt Vi. I'll be back in a minute."

Denny tilted his head. "So you're inclined to get lost?"

She shook her head. "I told her when we were parking out front that I hoped I could find my car come nightfall. That lot is packed."

"You're in safe hands. I have pretty good night vision." He winked. "And a flashlight in my car."

She smiled, and he noticed for the first time the dimple in her cheek. Sweet.

"Have you heard from your mother yet?"

"Not yet. Hopefully first thing tomorrow."

"And Todd's available?"

"We're having a meeting of the minds tomorrow. I'd like him to take the lead on getting the required permits and lining up his choice of crew. Getting the suppliers on board. This has to be a fast turnaround to wrap it up before your friend Barbie's wedding."

Ironically, the third weekend in October was Vic and Corrine's wedding day, too. Would they breathe a sigh of relief when they received his declined RSVP?

"I'm sorry that's creating pressure for you, Denny. I'm not trying to be difficult about not asking her to change locations, but this is an especially critical event we can't risk defaulting on."

"You and Viola are the experts on local land mines. I'll do my best, and it sounds as if you're sure Todd will do his."

"You're staying in Hunter Ridge until everything's done, right?"

Where had she gotten that idea?

"Once I'm assured of Todd's understanding of the project, I'll move on to responsibilities elsewhere. And check in regularly, of course."

In the background, the band's opening number rocked to a halt, and a fast-talking MC—his dad?—took the microphone and rattled off a welcome and details about the intended charity, door prizes and such. But Denny tuned it out when a troubled look passed through Lillian's eyes.

"Something wrong?" Surely after that quick rejection

of his non-invitation the other night, she wouldn't be sad to see him depart Hunter Ridge.

"Taylor. She's getting attached to you."

"That's okay. I don't mind her hanging around."

"What I mean is, she's going to be let down when you leave."

Then he remembered how her mother would come and go in and out of her life, and it felt like a mule kicked him.

"She's not *that* attached to me. There hasn't been enough time."

"Time enough."

"So you don't want her to hang out with me when I'm at the inn? She has her heart set on kicking down walls."

"I know. And I don't want to drive a wedge between you two. But I do ask that you be up-front and clear about how long you'll be staying. Don't let her get the impression that it's going to be longer than it is. Kids build things up in their minds. They have active dream worlds where everything works out the way they want it to."

Didn't he know it? But the fruitlessness of it finally gets hammered home and you focus on what you *can* control. Had Lillian been that way? Dreaming of a home and a relationship with her parents that they were incapable of providing? He'd been blown away to hear that her folks were well-known motivational speakers.

"I'll be careful around her." But he didn't like knowing a little kid was looking to him for something he couldn't deliver.

"Thank you." Lillian held his gaze for a long moment as if assessing his sincerity, then glanced anxiously around at the crowd. "Where did she get off to, anyway? I thought she said she'd be right back."

"She said she was helping your aunt Vi, so she's safe and sound."

"I'd better make sure. Hunter Ridge may be a small town, but that doesn't mean it isn't without its dangers. And events like this draw people from all over."

"She's fine, Lillian." Why the worry? Nobody would dare lay a hand on the kid with all the Hunters and their pals packed in around here.

"You don't—"

"Mister! They called your number! You won a cowboy hat!"

"Great!" Having absolutely no idea what he'd do with it, he nevertheless gave the excited little girl a half-hearted smile. He'd get laughed out of the office if he showed up in a cowboy hat.

Lillian had to admit that although Denny said he felt silly wearing it—and Taylor *insisted* he did—he looked good in the hat. He seemed more relaxed today than he had last week, too. Maybe the slower pace of Hunter Ridge was rubbing off on him?

While they didn't hang out together—she was still ever-conscious of the Friday evening gossip at the church—she found herself periodically searching him out in the crowd. He might be talking to his cousins or half siblings, aunts and uncles. Or helping haul in more chairs. They even had him serving up barbecue at one point. Leave it to the Hunters to work him into their big, loving family.

As nice as it was seeing the "long-lost Hunter" interact with family as day moved into nighttime, she couldn't help but feel a little jealous. She didn't know her own aunts, uncles or cousins well. Seldom saw her parents. And then there was Annalise.

What am I supposed to do about Taylor, Lord?

She glanced over at her niece, who was playing tic-tac-toe with Aunt Vi. Not romping and playing with the other kids taking part in organized potato sack and egg races. As usual, she'd stuck close throughout the afternoon, perking up when she glimpsed Denny as he passed by with a wink and a wave.

He didn't pause to speak to her niece, though, and Lillian knew that was her doing. Had she hurt his feelings by asking him to be cautious around Taylor? She didn't mean to come across as if she thought he'd deliberately and callously connected with her, knowing it would break her heart when he left.

"Aunt Lillian?" Taylor called over the rhythm of the band. "I think Aunt Viola is ready to go home."

The little girl nodded toward the elderly woman who, halfway through the Xs and Os, had fallen asleep in her chair.

Should she let her sleep awhile before waking her and attempting to get her out to the car? Earlier she'd suggested taking her home well before dark, but Aunt Viola protested, saying she was doing fine and enjoying herself.

Or had she said that because Todd had sat down with them to chat a bit, and she still had him at the top of her potentials list for her niece?

Taylor was looking a little drowsy, too.

Lillian got to her feet and held out her tote. "Will you please carry this for me, Taylor?" Then leaning down, she softly kissed Aunt Viola's forehead and her eyes fluttered open.

"We need to get Taylor home, Aunt Vi. Tomorrow's a school day."

"Oh, my, yes." She sat up with a slight grimace. "I can't believe I nodded off with that band blazing away. I must be getting old."

"Never."

Lillian helped her aunt to her feet, and they said their goodbyes to those at their table. She was relieved that once they reached the far edge of the patio, the walkway leading to the parking lot was lit by squat solar lights. Slipping her arm around her aunt's waist to steady her, she began the journey around the far side of the building.

She glanced up at the starry night sky and was thankful the earlier monsoon clouds had moved on without a deluge. A prayer of hope formed. If only she could get that permanent librarian position and the inn would become profitable. Then maybe she'd dare to seriously approach Annalise about custody. Adoption, even. She'd once hinted at it when Taylor was small. How she'd be happy to relieve her sister of the concern for a child. But Annalise had glibly thanked her for the offer and said she'd never saddle her older sister with full-time kid responsibilities.

Taylor wasn't a baby anymore, though. No longer a toddler easily passed back and forth. Her schoolwork and social skills with peers were both suffering—and right along with them, her ability to trust.

But if Annalise wouldn't cooperate? Was she justified in taking her own sister to court? Or would that attempt permanently shatter the sibling relationship—and Taylor be lost to her forever?

When they reached the dimly lit parking lot, they came to a halt. Shadowed cars were jammed in everywhere, even outside the huge graveled area. She wasn't about to wander around out there in search of the car with her aunt, who'd stumbled twice as they rounded the building. A quick search for her flashlight in the tote bag Taylor held proved fruitless.

"Aunt Vi, you and Taylor wait here. I'll go get the car. There are chairs on the porch if you need to sit down."

"I'm fine. Been sitting too long today anyway. It's made me stiff."

"Okay, then. I'll be right back."

Clicking the unlock button on her car key, she spotted the lights of her CR-V flash momentarily in the blackness of the sea of cars. At least she had a general idea of which direction to head. The towering pines that both lined and dotted the parking lot cast even darker shadows than the night sky. Where was the moon when you needed it?

Once deep in the maze of vehicles, she cautiously moved along, periodically flashing the vehicle's headlights. Mountain-size four-wheel-drive pickups and SUVs that were popular in this region didn't help her navigation skills, often blocking the guiding flash. She was rounding an extra-large pickup when she whacked her elbow on its back bumper, sending the key flying from her hand.

She let out a groan.

Please, Lord, help me find it. It would be nice to get Taylor and Aunt Vi home before dawn.

Having no idea how far the key had flown, she knelt to feel around in the gravel, panic rising. But the deep gloom cast by the hulking vehicles didn't help matters.

Now what?

"Lillian? Are you out here? Taylor thinks you're lost."

Denny. Closing her eyes momentarily with a silent

thank-you, she stood, spying a flashlight's gleam in the middle of the lot. "I'm over here."

When the beam swept the area, she raised both her arms and waved.

"Gotcha," he confirmed. "On my way."

She didn't dare leave the spot where she'd lost the key to join him, or she'd never hope to find it.

He zigzagged his way among the vehicles as she died a thousand deaths at him having to come to her rescue. When he finally entered the narrow space between the two massive pickups, his flashlight lowered to the ground.

"Aha. Found you. But you know, where I come from, we have a newfangled thing called streetlights. I know it might mean leaving the wagon-train era behind, but it might be something this tiny town should consider."

A comedian.

"Hunter Ridge is a designated Dark Sky City—one of many communities attempting to preserve the beauty of our night sky with lighting restrictions."

"I think they're succeeding," he said drily, and she could hear the smile in his voice. "You should have come and found me, though. Remember, I said I had a flashlight?"

"I remember. I thought I had one in my tote bag, too, but apparently not."

"All's well that ends well." He waved the flashlight's beam across the sea of shadowed vehicles. "Flash your car's headlights and let's go find it."

"I lost my key." She motioned to the ground. "Somewhere between these two big bruisers."

"Nice going."

Her face warmed at the teasing tone of his voice. "I hit my elbow on that truck and—"

"Gotta watch those parked trucks every second. They can be sneaky." His flashlight swept the ground between them. "Was it on a key chain? Brightly colored? Shiny?"

"Just the black-and-silver key. I'd taken it off the key chain so it would tuck more easily into my pocket."

"All right. Well, it's got to be here somewhere."

But after several minutes of fruitless searching, he moved to the end of the space between the trucks, got down on his belly and laid his head flat to the ground.

"What are you doing?" That sharp-edged gravel couldn't feel good.

He placed the flashlight on the ground and swept it slowly along the rocky surface. "Sometimes if you get down on the level of what you're looking for, you stand a better chance of finding it."

After two dozen slow sweeps of the light, she was ready to beg him to get up. But at that moment the beam halted. Then he wiggled it back and forth under one of the trucks.

"There you go. Right there. To the inside back of that front tire." He sat up, keeping the beam pinned on the object of his search. "See it?"

She hurried over and reached under the truck. Then, standing, she clasped the key gratefully to her heart before tucking it in her pocket and turning her face toward the night sky. "Thank You, Lord."

Denny chuckled as he joined her. "The Man Upstairs is good with a flashlight, is He?"

"As a matter of fact, He is—when He has a little help from His friends." She smiled up at Denny in the dim light of the flashlight, then gasped and instinctively raised her

"4 for 4" MINI-SURVEY

We are prepared to **REWARD** you with 2 FREE books and 2 FREE gifts for completing our MINI SURVEY!

FREE Value Over $20!

You'll get...

TWO FREE BOOKS & TWO FREE GIFTS

just for participating in our Mini Survey!

Dear Reader,

IT'S A FACT: if you answer 4 quick questions, we'll send you 4 FREE REWARDS!

I'm not kidding you. As a leading publisher of women's fiction, we value your opinions... and your time. That's why we are prepared to **reward** you handsomely for completing our mini-survey. In fact, we have 4 Free Rewards for you, including 2 free books and 2 free gifts.

As you may have guessed, that's why our mini-survey is called **"4 for 4".** Answer 4 questions and get 4 Free Rewards. It's that simple!

Thank you for participating in our survey,

Pam Powers

To get your 4 FREE REWARDS:
Complete the survey below and return the insert today to receive 2 FREE BOOKS and 2 FREE GIFTS guaranteed!

▼ DETACH AND MAIL CARD TODAY! ▼

"4 for 4" MINI-SURVEY

1 Is reading one of your favorite hobbies?
☐ YES ☐ NO

2 Do you prefer to read instead of watch TV?
☐ YES ☐ NO

3 Do you read newspapers and magazines?
☐ YES ☐ NO

4 Do you enjoy trying new book series with FREE BOOKS?
☐ YES ☐ NO

YES! I have completed the above Mini-Survey. Please send me my 4 FREE REWARDS (worth over $20 retail). I understand that I am under no obligation to buy anything, as explained on the back of this card.

❏ I prefer the regular-print edition
105/305 IDL GMYL

❏ I prefer the larger-print edition
122/322 IDL GMYL

FIRST NAME	LAST NAME

ADDRESS

APT.#	CITY

STATE/PROV.	ZIP/POSTAL CODE

READER SERVICE—Here's how it works:

hand to touch the side of his face. "You have gravel indentions. I think you're cut, too."

He obliviously scrubbed at his face with his free hand until she snagged it with her own. "Don't do that. You could make things worse."

"I'm not worried." A grin tugged at the corner of his mouth. "This mug has had worse done to it. Ask your good pastor."

He glanced down to where she still clasped his hand firmly in her own.

We're standing too close.

She could feel the warmth emanating from him. Smell the faint, masculine scent of his aftershave. They continued to stand together in the faint light, gazing into each other's eyes as though this were the most normal thing in the world to be doing. As if there were nothing they'd *rather* be doing.

"I— Thank you, Denny," she whispered. "For finding my key."

His gaze dropped momentarily to her lips, then back to her eyes, his voice low and husky. "Happy to help."

She swallowed, her heartbeat quickening, unable to pull her gaze from his.

"Taylor…" she said almost breathlessly, feeling herself sway toward him as she floundered for something to say. "Taylor will crown you a hero."

He tipped his head in quiet acknowledgment. "I can live with that. How—"

"Aunt Lillian! Mister! Where are you?"

At the sound of Taylor's voice bellowing across the parking lot, they immediately released hands and stepped back.

Her startled gaze met his, still intent on her.

Abruptly pulling out her key, she clicked it several times with shaking hands, flashing the CR-V's headlights and beeping the horn. Then she snatched the flashlight from Denny's big hand and took off in the direction of her vehicle.

Chapter Eight

"You aren't married, are you, Mister?"

He looked down at the pigtailed, overalls-clad girl who'd followed him out to the garden, where he intended to return a call from his GylesStyle assistant. For some reason, Lillian tended to frown when he took or placed calls unrelated to the Pinewood project, so he'd taken to slipping out of sight and earshot when his real life needed attention.

"Do you think I *look* married?" he teased.

Taylor scowled in concentration. "I don't know."

"What does married look like?"

Come on, Den, stop kidding the little thing. She probably has a crush on you. Wants to marry you when she grows up.

She studied him. "You don't have a ring, right?"

He waggled the fingers of his left hand. "Nope. No ring."

That seemed to satisfy her, for she took off running back to the inn. He smiled as he punched Betsy's speed-dial number.

"Bets. What's up?"

"Sorry to bother you, but I thought you should know that Vic fired Craig this morning."

"Not funny."

Betsy was known for starting her calls off with something outrageous, so when she got to the real reason for the call, it didn't seem overly calamitous.

"I'm serious. They got into a big fight in Craig's office this morning. I could hear it clear down the hall. Vic fired him on the spot."

"Is he out of his mind?" Denny paced the patio. Craig had more experience at GylesStyle in his little finger than Vic could ever hope to accumulate in a lifetime.

"Could you hear what the argument was about? What set Vic off?" He'd always had a powder-keg temper, but to fire Craig, of all people? That was akin to cutting off your own right arm.

"It was about—" She paused.

"Spit it out, Bets."

"It was about *you*."

Denny stilled. "What about me?"

"I couldn't hear it all. Just bits and pieces because sometimes it got eerily quiet in there, and I thought maybe one of them had dropped the other off the high-rise's balcony. But part of it at least had to do with changes Vic wanted him to make, and Craig was digging in his heels. He said *you* would never make such a foolhardy decision, and he wasn't going to do it without consulting you first. That's when Vic fired him."

With a groan, Denny lowered himself to a nearby stone bench.

"Then Vic charged out of the office, his face all red, and not long after that Craig left, too. I don't know if for good or to cool off."

"When did this happen?"

"Maybe an hour ago."

"Thanks for letting me know. Keep me in the loop if you hear anything else."

"Will do."

He immediately checked his phone messages. Nothing from his buddy. He punched his colleague's number, but it went straight to voice mail. "Craig. I talked to Betsy. Call me."

Still stunned, he stared, unseeing, across the garden in the direction of the gazebo. If Vic started off deliberately provoking Craig, how long would it be before he went after others on Denny's core team? Nathan? Elijah? Felicia? The rest?

"Denny?"

As if in a fog, he looked toward the inn, where Lillian stood at the back door.

"Todd's here."

"Be there in a minute."

With his mother's enthusiastic approval last week, the Pinewood's show was officially on the road. Todd and his crew were on board, and they'd collaborated late into the night all the previous week, firming up plans. If all went well, permits would go to approval the first of next week—a major advantage to a small town, having a local contractor driving things. It didn't hurt, either, being associated with the influential Hunter clan himself. Big ducks in a little pond.

Lillian turned as if to go back inside, but changed her mind and headed in his direction. "Is everything okay?"

He must look as bad as he felt to elicit that remark. He had no intention of discussing what had taken place at GylesStyle, but at least she wasn't avoiding him as she had since that episode in the Hunter's Hideaway parking lot a week ago yesterday. In retrospect, he still didn't know exactly what had happened there. But it certainly wasn't about a lost car key.

He shoved back the memory of her star-kissed face upturned to his and abruptly rose to his feet. "A minor business glitch. I'll get it worked out."

"It isn't easy, though, is it, doing the work here at the inn when you need to be—want to be—elsewhere?"

She had no idea. "Nobody ever said life was easy."

"No. But you seem to be a man who likes being in control."

"Come again?"

"Never mind. It's none of my business. Something I've observed."

"Doesn't everyone like to feel he's the master of his fate?"

"I suppose. But it's kind of an illusion, isn't it? When it comes right down to it, there's little we're in control of, although we can control our attitude and may be able to influence some outcomes, especially when we team up with God. And that's where the trust factor comes into play. But it's a bigger struggle for some to come to that realization than for others."

"And you think I'm one of those?"

"It's clear you don't like it when your hands are pried off the wheel and someone else is steering."

She must have wiretapped that last phone call.

"So I can't help but wonder," she continued, "*why* you're still here, Denny, now that you have a contractor lined up. It's obvious Hunter Ridge is the last place on earth you want to be."

"I'm assisting my mother because I love her, and this

project brings her pleasure." *And her husband's being a jerk to hold my career hostage.* "It so happens that right now, keeping up with things on two fronts is taking extra time and effort. But I've juggled my share of conflicting deadlines in the past. It will work out."

And it would, if Vic didn't sabotage everything Denny had worked hard for. "You said Todd's here?"

"And a couple of movers with a big truck."

"With your few guests now situated elsewhere— Viola said they seemed quite pleased with their alternate accommodations—I told the movers we'd temporarily transfer everything, except Viola's apartment, which will come later, to a storage facility here in town. I doubt there's much we'll keep, but it will be out of the way until we decide how to dispose of it."

"A secondhand store, maybe. Or Goodwill. But I do like the daylight coming in with the window treatments gone."

He'd hired a few high-school kids—his cousin Luke's son and daughter and their friends—who came in after school the previous day to strip the beds, take down the drapes and pictures, roll up rugs, and box knickknacks and other miscellaneous items.

"Todd's extended crew placed the orders for a new furnace, water heaters, appliances and cabinetry. Then we can make selections on the decorating side while Todd and company move on the structural changes."

Not that he didn't think her capable of doing that, but he didn't want to see her lavish, ultrafeminine designs slipping in there when he wasn't looking. And could he help it if he enjoyed her company?

Lillian cut him an anxious look as they headed back to the inn. "It's six weeks until Barbie's wedding. That hit me hard when I woke up this morning. Do you think a project of this magnitude can be done by then?"

With a GylesStyle team, no doubt about it. But he had no idea with Todd Samuels. There were many unknowns, despite tapping into a few of the usual suppliers he'd worked with in the past. As much as he joked about it, this wasn't a reality TV program where you could manipulate the end result with tape splices and scene retakes.

Kicking down a wall was just the beginning.

"I can't make promises. Stuff happens. But we aren't trying to pull off anything fancy like on TV. We're sticking to the basics—general repairs, new insulation, electrical and plumbing upgrades. Those take time, but we'll give it all we've got."

He still didn't fully understand why keeping this Barbie Gray's wedding at the inn was so all-fired important. But then, he didn't know much about the ins and outs of small-town goings-on. He'd always heard little communities were microcosms of the larger world around them, but intensely more personal. He didn't know his next-door neighbors in the condo high-rise where he lived and couldn't imagine them taking a personal interest in his business, let alone influencing it.

He shuddered at the thought.

After walking Lillian to the back door of the inn, he held it open for her. "Hey, guess who I saw this morning. Chicken Man."

"Oh…really?"

"Yeah, shooting baskets with a couple of other teens outside the school. Seemed normal enough. In fact, I saw him last evening, too, when I stopped off at the hardware store. He was chatting with the checkout clerk."

"His father owns the store, and he works there part-time stocking shelves."

"I find it intriguing, though." Denny playfully tapped Lillian's arm. "Seems it's only when I'm with you that he puts on an Oscar-winning performance."

She placed her hand to her heart. "I can't tell you how special that makes me feel."

"Maybe you bring out the best in him." He chuckled as he followed her inside. Then, even though he hadn't felt his phone vibrate, he surreptitiously checked his messages.

Nothing from Craig.

Although Denny didn't seem to be getting as many business call interruptions as he had the first week he arrived, he seemed to be more on edge today than any day previously. Lillian had hoped, having seen him interacting with his family on Labor Day, that being away from the city was having a mellowing effect. If so, it hadn't lasted long.

From the apartment kitchen table, where, after work, she'd placed her laptop to do online searches, she glanced over at Taylor, who'd flopped on the floor in front of the TV. She had the closed captioning on and sound turned off so she wouldn't bother Aunt Viola, who was in her room reviewing favorite recipes and brainstorming new breakfast menus for the inn's reopening. "What are you watching?"

"That bride dress show."

Again? Lillian shook her head as she scrolled down on the laptop to find a perfect match to the bedspread in Denny's sketches.

"Do you like this one, Aunt Lillian?" Taylor pointed to the screen.

She leaned over in her chair to see better. "It's pretty on her, but too poufy for me."

"What did *your* wedding dress look like? I don't remember it."

As much as she'd like to think that day had been overlooked by Taylor, who'd arrived a few days beforehand, that would be too much to hope for.

"It was white. Lacy. With a veil." She'd found it at a shop in Canyon Springs.

"Where is it now?"

"I sold it, so I don't have it anymore."

"I wish you'd have kept it." Taylor grabbed the remote and flipped off the TV, then plopped down in a chair next to Lillian. Propping her elbows on the table and her face in her hands, she sighed. "How come you didn't marry that guy?"

Keep it simple. Kids want simple.

"I prayed about it and realized he wasn't the man God wanted me to marry."

There, that was easy.

Taylor thought for a moment. "How come you didn't pray about it until your wedding day?"

"I did, but…maybe I wasn't listening for His answer."

"My mom's never been married, either."

"No, she hasn't."

Taylor slipped from her chair and moved to the window looking out on the sunset-illuminated garden. "She has lots of boyfriends, though. Do you have boyfriends, Aunt Lillian?"

"Not at the moment."

Her niece looked back over her shoulder. "Do you want one?"

"Maybe someday."

"Why not now?"

"Because…this time I'm trying hard to listen for God's answer."

Taylor nodded her understanding. "So you don't have to sell any more wedding dresses."

"Exactly." She didn't want to give her niece the impression that not marrying her fiancé was shameful, but a word of caution was in order, especially since Taylor and Denny seemed to be becoming thick. "Sweetie, please don't discuss my almost-wedding with anyone else. It's between you and me. Okay?"

"Okay."

"So how's it coming out here?" Aunt Viola stepped out of her room. "Getting your shopping done?"

"I'm bookmarking items I think fit our concept, then will get Denny's input to ensure I'm on track and within budget."

"He should turn the whole thing over to you and focus his attention elsewhere."

"He keeps his finger in the pie on most things." That controlling trait again. She tried not to take it personally, but if he had so much to do here and at his real job, why not divvy up more responsibilities? Delegate the decision-making?

"I guess we'll be seeing a lot of Todd from now on?" Her aunt sounded hopeful.

"Probably so." Lillian kept her tone light. Neutral. And her eyes on the computer screen.

"You should fix him one of those slow-cooked, melt-in-your-mouth Italian beef sandwiches you have such a knack with. You know what they say. The way to a man's heart is—"

"Let's not go there." She gave her aunt a warning look, aware that Taylor was still at the window, all ears. But just then the little girl spun toward her.

"Mister's in the garden. Can I go out, too?"

She should say no. Discourage further bonding between the pair, but at the hopeful gleam in her niece's eyes, she didn't have the heart to deny the request.

"That's fine. But come in when it gets dark. And if Denny's working, don't bother him, okay?"

"I won't." Then she hit the door running.

Aunt Vi pulled up a chair at the table. "She thinks a lot of Denny."

She didn't need her aunt getting on her case about that. "I've already spoken to him."

"About what?"

"About being careful of letting her get too attached. He won't be staying long, and I don't want her to get her heart broken."

"Or *your* heart broken."

Lillian stiffened as the awkward encounter in the Hideaway's parking lot flashed through her mind for the millionth time. Although she enjoyed Denny's company, that was an embarrassing fluke. Nothing was going on between them.

"Yes, if he hurts her that will certainly hurt me, too."

"You know that's not what I meant. You like him. Which is why you're not giving Todd the time of day, isn't it?"

"Don't be ridiculous."

"Denny's likable, don't you think? Responsible. Good

with kids. Good-looking, too. If I were fifty years younger, I'd give you a run for your money."

"In case you haven't noticed, he's way too much like Cameron."

"He's nothing like Cameron. Where did you get that idea?"

"He's wed to his cell phone and can't wait to get back to the big city."

Aunt Vi scoffed. "He's a man who doesn't know any better because he hasn't yet seen any better. But I think Hunter Ridge is starting to grow on him. As are you, if I'm not mistaken. He has a contractor to oversee things now, but he's not making any more noises about leaving as I'd expected he would. *Something* is keeping him here."

"I don't know where you get that idea." Lillian clicked the mouse to select another page on the screen. "Besides, it's too soon after that fiasco with Cameron for me to consider another relationship. Three months ago I was set to pledge my life to someone I thought God had picked out. I no longer trust my own judgment when it comes to men, except to recognize what's certain to be a no-win situation if I were to involve myself with another city-minded man."

"I thought you enjoyed that trip you and one of your gal friends took to San Francisco a few years ago. You couldn't stop talking about the city—the shopping, the seals on the docks, the harbor cruises and those clam-chowder bread bowls."

"A week there is not the same as living there."

"You liked Boston when you visited there, too." Aunt Viola's eyes narrowed. "Be honest with me, Lillian. If Taylor and I had been out of the picture when Cameron

came along, when he jumped at that job offer in Bean-
town would you have married him? Or left him at the
altar because you loathed leaving Hunter Ridge?"

How many times had she asked herself that very question? "Honestly? I don't know. But I'm thankful I didn't
marry him. I think that at the time Cameron came into
my life last February, I was acutely conscious that my
next birthday would be my thirtieth. My biological clock
was ticking loudly, and then there he was. An answered
prayer."

"Or not."

"Or not." Lillian got up and moved to the window to
brush back the curtain and look out on Denny having an
animated conversation with her niece. Definitely storybook worthy, with those broad shoulders and a generous
smile as he gave his full attention to Taylor.

At that moment, though, he glanced toward the window and saw her standing there. Waved. Taylor turned
and waved, too. Lillian smiled and lifted her own hand.
Then let the curtain fall back.

"So you can see," she ended lamely as she returned to
her laptop, "why I can no longer trust my own judgment."

"You say that, but—" Her aunt rose and moved to the
kitchen, then looked thoughtfully at Lillian. "I'm wondering if it's not only your heart you're not trusting, but
God, as well."

"Fancy meeting you here."

Seeing Lillian was just the thing he needed after talking to Craig, who'd insisted Denny not get in the middle
of his dispute with Vic. He was going straight to Elden
and wanted to handle it himself.

Yet while her presence was welcome, Lillian was the

last person Denny expected to run into at the hardware store over the lunch hour. They'd hardly seen each other in the past week, having taken to texting as a means of communication. She looked taken aback to see him, as well.

"Are we here for the same thing?" She held up a handful of interior paint samples. Sand, Navajo white, pale parchment. "I was about to text you to see if you agreed a warm white would be better than a cool one. I've looked online, but sometimes the colors aren't true. They can vary from computer to computer."

"I'm going with warm, too." He held up a dozen samplings of wood stains he'd picked up when he first hit the store—weathered oak, golden pecan—then got distracted by lighting fixtures. "We should probably make our selections together to make certain we have a match."

"Once we've narrowed them down, we can get a small can of each and paint a big swatch on a wall and stain a board to see how we like them side by side."

"You saw that on one of those do-it-yourself shows, didn't you?" he teased as he handed her the wood stain samples. "Or is that something all pretty small-town girls are born knowing?"

"Very funny. But hey, if it works, why not go for it? You can't tell much with these tiny samples."

"That's for sure."

"What do you have there?" She pointed at two folding display boards he gripped in his other hand.

"Flooring samples. I was told I could take these with me if I brought them back tomorrow."

"Hardwood flooring in the entry, parlor, library, office, dining room and bedrooms. Tile in the kitchen, laundry, storage rooms and breakfast nook, right?"

"Good memory."

Together they walked to the front of the store, out the exit and onto the sidewalk. He drew to a halt, not willing to scale their communication back to texting just yet. It was a blue-skied autumn day, the scent of sun-warmed pine filling his senses, and Lillian was looking lovely in an emerald turtleneck sweater and skirt.

"Our paths," he ventured, "haven't crossed much lately. You must be keeping busy."

"The library, mostly. And when I'm not buried on the job, I'm trying to keep out from underfoot of Todd and his crew as much as possible. Taylor isn't making a bother of herself when I'm not there, is she? Aunt Vi's oversight can be lax at times, and there are several hours between when my niece gets home from school and I get away from work."

"She's been no problem at all. I let her help me kick through a wall upstairs between those two bedrooms we're converting to a single." He squinted one eye. "But don't tell me you're a helicopter mom."

"I'm not a *mom* at all."

"Maybe not by birth, but Taylor looks to you in that role. I've noticed she's minding you better now than she did a few weeks ago, just as you thought would happen once the immediacy of her mother's visit faded."

"It's always an adjustment for both of us when her mother pops in or drops her off. Annalise isn't much of a disciplinarian. No set bedtimes. No staying on top of homework. Too much TV and junk food. I get to be the bad guy each time my sister takes off with her and then drops her off again."

"Taylor doesn't consider you a bad guy at all. Far from

it. In fact, she's always telling me how wonderful you are. Smart. Pretty. A great cook. How much fun you are."

He could be mistaken, but he was beginning to suspect the cute grade-schooler was trying to set him up with her aunt. Who, incidentally, didn't seem to find him of particular interest.

It was a blow to the old ego.

Lillian laughed. "Laying it on thick, is she? Her birthday is coming up—I wonder what she's setting me up to ask for."

"A birthday, huh? I'll keep that in mind and will take everything she tells me with a grain of salt. How old? Seven? Eight?"

"Eight."

"From what I've seen, you're doing a great job with her."

"Thanks." She took a step back. "I'm afraid I need to get back to the library. It was good seeing you."

"You, too." But when she moved off in the direction of the library, preferring to walk as usual, he couldn't help but call after her. "Should we get together tonight?"

She halted and looked in his direction, a cautious curiosity lighting her eyes.

"I mean to narrow down the colors—with your aunt, too, of course."

"Daylight would be better for that, don't you think?"

"Noon tomorrow, then? I can pick up sandwiches and we can make it a working lunch out in the garden."

She hesitated for the briefest moment, then nodded. "Okay, sure. I'll see you then."

For whatever reason, Denny whistled a merry tune on the way to his car, not in all that much of a hurry at the moment to get himself out of Hunter Ridge.

Chapter Nine

"Reba won't do half as good a job as you'd do," Aunt Viola assured her niece as Lillian poured three glasses of lemonade in preparation for lunch with Denny.

She'd thought he'd be here by now, knowing how quickly a lunch hour flew by.

"So don't be concerned," her aunt continued, "that she's real competition for the position."

It was now fact rather than rumor that Reba Clancy intended to apply. But the timing stank. What chance did she have of landing the job now that the other woman's return was imminent?

"But she's a widowed former local girl," Lillian reminded her aunt as she put the pitcher back in the refrigerator. "With Reba growing up here and everyone knowing her family, that will count for something with the library advisory board."

And Reba didn't publicly dump the grandson of one of those board members.

Aunt Vi snorted, not something that the well-mannered former librarian was often given to doing. "As I recall, she couldn't wait to ditch this town as soon as they handed her that high-school diploma. Now that her daughter and son-in-law moved here to get away from the Mile-High City, she suddenly finds our community hits the spot."

"I can understand the appeal."

"Well, you deserve the job and I think I should have something to say about it since I held down the fort for decades."

While Lillian appreciated her aunt's vote of confidence, in reality Reba had considerably more experience than Lillian and was taking an extra-early retirement from a library in Denver to move closer so she could enjoy her grandkids. No doubt the position interested her as much as it did Lillian, and for the same reasons. She wanted to work and live in Hunter Ridge.

Lillian glanced at her aunt, who was now gazing thoughtfully out the window at the garden. Despite attempts to rally, the older woman's spirits had faltered noticeably after learning for certain that Reba would be throwing her hat into the ring. Without the full-time position, could Lillian hope to keep her family in Hunter Ridge?

"Anybody home?"

Lillian had left the apartment door open, and Denny's voice echoed from the front entry. The place was so quiet when Todd's crew left the premises for their lunch break or at the end of a workday.

Denny appeared in the doorway. "Sorry I'm late. You wouldn't believe the line at the grocery-store deli." He set down the display boards, then held up three white bags. "I brought you something, too, Viola."

"Aren't you sweet."

Lillian stood and gathered up the paint and wood stain samples she'd been sorting on the table. "Should we head outside? I need to be back at the library in forty-five minutes."

"You two go on ahead." Aunt Vi took one of the bags from Denny. "I need to call and check on a friend."

"Once we narrow down the selections, you can give us your opinion," Lillian assured her aunt with a concerned glance at her. Was she truly intending to place a phone call, or was she not feeling well and planned to lie down and rest?

Outside they chose a gazebo table where Lillian placed glasses of lemonade before spreading out the interior finish samples between the two of them.

"They're already making great headway, but it's awfully quiet around here when the crew's out, isn't it?" Denny pulled wrapped sandwiches from the bags and handed her one, then split open a package of chips and placed it where they could be reached. "I hope smoked turkey suits you."

"Perfect, thanks." She gazed around the secluded garden, acutely conscious that she was sharing a private lunch with the man who just last week she and her aunt had been discussing. Of course she liked Denny. Who wouldn't? But her aunt was way off base with her romantic speculation. "I'm not around much during the day, but I enjoy hearing the crew at work. Their banter and laughter. Then at the end of the day when they leave, I always go through the house and poke around in nooks and crannies they've exposed in the walls."

"Looking for—?"

"The Newell family treasure."

"Ah, right. Forgot."

"You don't think there's anything to it, do you? You just think it's a silly family fabrication."

"Who am I to judge? I just question what kind of 'treasure' someone in a town like this would have that needed hiding. A pinecone collection? Butterflies?" He leaned forward, his gaze suddenly intent. "Your great-great-granddaddy wasn't Al Capone, was he?"

She laughed. "Not to my knowledge. And like I said earlier, nobody knows anything about it except that my great-great-grandfather once made reference to the so-called treasure's existence."

Taking a bite of her sandwich, she chewed, then swallowed before pushing three paint samples in his direction. "What do you think of these?"

"I like the lightest one. What about you?"

"Same here. We'll have to put window treatments up for privacy and warmth, but a light paint should help counter that."

He nodded. "I'm good with it. How about the stain for the doors and woodwork?"

She took a sip of lemonade. "I'm thinking the interior doors, trim and baseboards should be painted the same color as the walls. Then we can stain the window frames."

"That would help open it up visually."

"I'd like to avoid having the hardwood floors be that nearly black tone that's popular on the renovation shows. I can't help but think that a few years from now it will be passé, and everyone will start ripping them out or covering them up with another kind of treatment. Besides, it's way too dark for the look we're trying to establish in here."

He helped himself to a chip. "I completely agree."

"You're certainly mellow today. Sure you're feeling well?"

"Feeling great."

"Hunter Ridge must be rubbing off on you." She reached again for her sandwich. "Listened to any crickets lately?"

He grinned and shook his head. "Just feeling good today, I guess. Must be the company I'm keeping."

Surely he didn't mean hers?

"So you've spent time with your family while you've been here, then?"

"Some. I've had several nice chats with Grandma Jo, Aunt Elaine and Uncle Dave. I usually stop by the inn in the evening to pick up something to call dinner and generally see somebody I'm related to in one way or another. But it's not like they're all over me. They're giving me breathing room."

"You need that?"

He nodded. "I may bear the name Hunter, but I'm pretty much a stranger to them and them to me. I'm not convinced that it's time well spent to try to worm my way into their midst when I should be focusing on work at the inn."

"It's a shame not to take advantage of being close to family when you're in their backyard, so to speak. You know, like time with your dad."

Denny chuckled. "You mean my ultrasensitive father who didn't think twice about loudly and publicly sharing his heartfelt condolences that his son had been dumped at the altar three months ago?"

Lillian's breath caught. This was the first time Denny had made reference to that, acknowledging he knew she'd heard his father's tactless comment.

"I'm sorry about your breakup. That had to be hard." She hated to think of him grieving his fiancée's abrupt departure. But then again, as she knew all too well, there was always more to the story. "If you don't mind my asking, where is she now? Do you still keep in contact with her?"

She was curious how other couples dealt with a situation like that. Cameron wanted nothing to do with her. He'd cut all ties.

"Not directly. I did recently receive an invitation to Corrine and Vic's upcoming wedding, though."

She frowned as she played through the little Denny had told her about his life in San Francisco, then gasped. "Vic. You don't mean your *stepbrother* Vic, do you?"

"That's the one." He popped a chip in his mouth.

"He's marrying your fiancée?"

"Former fiancée."

"How could he do that to you?"

Denny offered a shrug and a smile. "You've heard of all's fair in love and—"

"You find it humorous?"

"It turned out for the best."

"How can you say that? And how can a brother show such little respect for you?"

Annalise didn't always have a high opinion of her big sister, but she'd never betray her like that.

Which was worse—never to have gained Vic's respect, or to have thought all these years that he had Elden's, only to discover that may have been a grand self-delusion?

"In retrospect, Corrine and I weren't that great of a match."

It wasn't that they didn't get along. But he could now see that their underlying motivation for the relationship was more about what the other could bring to the table. Almost like a business partnership. Or a political alliance. His growing professional reputation and connection to the prestigious Gyles family increased her social status. And he'd counted on her head-turning looks and people savvy to help smooth the corporate climb for him.

"I know it's hard to understand," he continued, "how two people could get to their wedding day not recognizing that theirs wasn't a match made in heaven. But take it from me—in the long run it's been more humiliating than heartbreaking."

What would Lillian think of that confession?

"It must have been difficult, though, to have someone claim to love you," she said in a small voice, "then publicly turn her back on you."

"It wasn't the high point of my day, no."

"I'm sorry, Denny. You didn't deserve that."

He shrugged. "I'd like to think I didn't, but I've never claimed to be perfect. From what she texted me that morning as I stood at the front of the church, she'd belatedly figured that out. 'You are a hard man to love, Hayden Harrison Hunter.'"

A whimper escaped Lillian's lips. "That's awful."

"But a truth that was direct and to the point."

She was silent a long moment, and he saw her sneak a look at her watch. So much for a working lunch, with him blathering on about Corrine doing him wrong like some popular Nashville singer.

"While I've never been left at the altar," she said carefully, "I do know what it's like to break up with someone you thought you were committing to."

"A longtime boyfriend?"

"A fiancé, actually."

"You were engaged? I'm sorry you had to go through that, Lillian. The guy had to be an idiot to let a woman like you get away from him."

She gave him an uncomfortable look. "It's sweet of you to say that, but you hardly know me."

"I'm a good judge of character, though. I'm especially impressed with your love for your aunt and Taylor. Any kid would be fortunate to have you in their corner."

Likely any man, too, which made him resent her former fiancé. He couldn't imagine a guy in his right mind breaking up with Lillian, deliberately hurting her.

"So what happened?" She'd asked him personal questions. Turnabout was fair play, right?

After a long silence, when he was almost ready to say "never mind" and apologize, she spoke.

"I met Cameron here in Hunter Ridge when I came to see to Aunt Viola's care after she broke her hip."

That was this year. Whoa.

"If you don't want to talk about it, that's okay. I didn't realize it was something so recent."

"You shared." She offered a faltering smile. "I can, too."

He nodded for her to go on.

"He'd been working in Boston, but lost his job and returned to his hometown to start fresh. It was a classic whirlwind romance. The wedding was set for the first Saturday in June." Same day as he was to marry Corrine. "I'd quit my job in Phoenix, where I'd already taken a leave of absence, and we were making plans to call Hunter Ridge our home for the rest of our lives."

"And then?"

"And then... Annalise dropped Taylor off a few days before the wedding."

Denny winced. "He didn't want the kid around?"

"Or Aunt Viola."

"So he walked? I'm sorry, Lillian. This is…" He shook his head.

He and Lillian had more in common than he'd have ever guessed. He was willing to admit that while it hadn't been a lot of fun, he in some ways deserved what Corrine had done to him. But what that idiot did to Lillian? No way did she deserve that.

"You're well rid of him, and never think differently."

"Thank you."

As if only just realizing she'd made such a personal confession to someone she'd recently met, Lillian wrapped up the remainder of her sandwich and stuffed it in her tote bag, then stood.

"I'm late getting back to work."

He stood, as well. "Did you walk? I can drive you."

"No, thanks. I— No, thank you. I'm a fast walker. I'll make up the time at the end of the day or go in early tomorrow." She glanced down at the table. "Thank you for bringing lunch. And feel free to get sample cans and paint big swatches of our color choices to confirm, and get Aunt Vi's opinion, too."

"Lillian—"

"Gotta run. See you later."

For the remainder of the afternoon until quitting time, Lillian's head pounded, and she was grateful that it was a slow afternoon. Jeri was out, and she didn't have to expend energy on small talk or anything much other than checking out and reshelving books.

She hadn't lied to Denny. Not exactly. But she hadn't told the whole story, either. Why not get it over with and stop living in fear that he'd hear about her role in the breakup from someone else?

But learning how Denny felt on the other end of being left standing at the church brideless brought home again what she'd done to Cameron. Had Cameron loved her at all? Had she broken his heart? Or had he, as in Denny's situation, been more humiliated than desolate? Of course, Denny's shrug-off was most likely a front he'd put on, unwilling to admit that a woman he'd cared for telling him he was difficult to love had hurt. Deeply.

The timing was the same as her own situation—a mere three months ago. No wonder he kept himself so busy, buried in work. He probably didn't want to think about what happened that day any more than she liked thinking about her own almost-wedding.

"One that *I* canceled," she said under her breath as she slipped another book into its spot on the shelf.

Everyone in town knew what she'd done—except Denny Hunter.

So it was with great relief that for the next week she was able to focus on her job at the library, picking up extra hours from another part-timer who'd gone on vacation and returning predominantly to communicating with Denny by text.

It took tricky maneuvering to keep what she was doing from being obvious. But despite extensive collaboration on furniture selection, website and brochure ideas, and how to deliver the best experience for future guests, she managed to elude one-on-one time with him. Thankfully, she'd taken advantage of the presence of Todd's crew with their increasingly lengthy hours, as well as Aunt Viola's and Taylor's company.

And yet…while Denny's texts were often cute and clever, she missed spending time alone with him.

Taylor's birthday was fast approaching, and Lillian

and Aunt Viola had decided on a party with a handful of classmates who were most often in Taylor's sphere at school and church. To Lillian's relief, while not actually Taylor's *friends*, at least they were a step above generic schoolmates.

The party was only two days away, and her niece seemed to be settling down. But how much of that was due to Lillian's efforts rather than to Denny's undivided attention whenever they saw each other? Taylor clearly cared about him, and if she wasn't mistaken, her feelings were returned tenfold.

So odd. Denny hadn't initially struck her as a family-man type. A lover of kids. And yet he welcomed her niece at every opportunity and had even pulled himself away from work to attend several of her soccer games. Amazingly, he hadn't so much as glanced at his cell phone while there to cheer her on.

But unexpected or not, Lillian wasn't about to look a gift horse in the mouth, grateful for how Taylor seemed to be further adjusting. Lillian had promised her that tonight, following dinner and after they dropped off Aunt Viola at the church for a Bible study, they'd make cupcakes. Thankfully, despite a phone call from Barbie demanding that the accent colors on the reception tables be changed—again forgetting that was the caterer's sphere— Lillian was relaxed and ready to spend the evening with her niece.

"Be careful, there." Lillian took Aunt Viola's favorite big mixing bowl from Taylor, who had climbed up on a step stool to claim it from a cabinet.

"I get to lick the bowl," the little girl announced once she reached the bottom step and hopped excitedly to the floor.

"You not only get to lick it, you get to pour in the ingredients, mix them and put them in the cupcake tins."

Taylor clapped her hands as Lillian retrieved the eggs, milk and other makings for several dozen of the treats and set them on the table where her niece could reach them. These days she seemed to be in higher spirits, happier, more like the little girl she'd once been. To Lillian's delight, she and her niece had drawn closer as the weeks since her mother's last visit faded into the past.

Would Annalise put in an appearance for Taylor's birthday?

The possibility was troubling. Things were going so well right now. And yet Annalise *was* Taylor's mother. She had a right to celebrate a special day with her daughter. Surprisingly, though, Taylor hadn't speculated on that possibility. At least not aloud. Did she want her mother to come, but was afraid to get her hopes up?

Lillian had left the door to the apartment open, enjoying the chatter of Todd's work crew as they wrapped things up after an extra-long day.

Todd was going above and beyond the call of duty for the Pinewood Inn. Yes, he was being paid well, but he doted on Aunt Viola, who was a good friend of his grandmother. And maybe doted a little on *her*, too?

The ongoing renovation would be a perfect opportunity for them to get to know each other better. She did enjoy his company and sense of humor, and admired his work ethic. But despite Aunt Viola's high hopes, there had never been that acute awareness on her part when he stepped into the room, that *zing* such as she'd felt with—

"I get to crack the eggs," a familiar male voice called from the apartment's open doorway.

Zing.

Taylor squealed. "Mister!"

She dashed across the room to where he swung her into his strong arms and carried her into the kitchen. "What are we making here, ladies?"

"Birthday cupcakes! And you can help."

As he set Taylor on her feet, his eyes smiled uncertainly into Lillian's, clearly questioning if he was welcome. Maybe her ploys to avoid him hadn't been as subtle as she'd convinced herself they were?

Her heart pounding erratically, she motioned to the table laden with everything needed for the baking extravaganza. "The more the merrier."

He grinned. "Show me what to do."

"First we need aprons." Taylor opened a drawer of Aunt Viola's finest. Lillian rarely wore an apron for cooking and felt rather old-fashioned when Taylor tied one covered with hearts around her waist, and a floral one around Denny's.

"I get the one with bunnies on it," the little girl announced, backing up to Denny so he could tie hers in a big bow. Then she rabbit-hopped to the table. "Let's go!"

For over an hour, they took turns adding ingredients, mixing, filling red-and-white polka-dot baking cups with batter, and sliding the cupcake tins into a preheated oven, laughing the whole time.

"Can we frost them tonight, Aunt Lillian? Some of them are cool."

"It's getting late, and someone will be dropping off Aunt Vi pretty soon. We should probably get this mess taken care of before she gets home, or you know she'll jump in and try to do the cleaning up."

"I wanted to frost them tonight. Please?" She looked

up at Denny in appeal. "You can stay to frost them, can't you, Mister?"

His gaze met Lillian's as it had countless times that evening. Smiling. Laughing.

Questioning.

"It's up to you," she responded to his unspoken query. "We can get started on the frosting in the fifteen to twenty minutes it takes this last batch to bake."

"Do I get to lick the bowl?" He cut a teasing look in her niece's direction.

Her smile wider than ever, Taylor took his hand. "You can *share* the bowl with me."

"Then let's do it."

Lillian pulled two more tins of golden cupcakes from the oven and placed them on stoneware trivets, then slid the last batch in.

By the time they finished, she'd received a call from Aunt Viola that she'd be running late. The ladies' group decided to take additional time to discuss the church's annual Christmas project—brightening the season for unwed mothers in the region.

With a little coaxing, Lillian got Taylor to the bathroom and filled the tub with enough bubbles that she could play as she bathed. Leaving the door open a crack and promising to check on her in a few minutes, she returned to the kitchen to find Denny up to his elbows in dishwater.

"You could have used the dishwasher."

"It's full of dirty dishes. I couldn't squeeze these big bowls or tins in there."

"My bad. I should have run it after dinner. Here, I can dry."

They worked in quiet companionship for a few minutes, Lillian keeping her ears tuned to the splashing and a happy song Taylor sang from the tub.

Denny angled a look at her. "I haven't seen you around much."

So he *had* noticed. Was that why he'd turned up here unannounced?

"I could say the same for you. Between this project and your real job, I imagine you're up to your eyeballs."

"Pretty much." He scrubbed another cupcake tin, then handed it to her. "Taylor seemed to have a good time tonight. I can see a big difference in her since the day she garnered the courage to sell me a barbecue ticket."

"Things are going great." She dried the tin and set it aside. "Maybe too great."

"What do you mean?"

"I haven't heard anything from my sister, Annalise, for weeks. Not a peep. That leads me to believe she may decide to surprise Taylor on her birthday."

He dried his hands on his apron, untied it and then placed it on the counter. "Which means starting from ground zero all over again."

She pulled a magnetized photo frame from the front of the refrigerator to gaze down at it. Taylor and Annalise.

"Your sister?"

She nodded. "I know I shouldn't be like this. I feel so selfish. But I don't want her messing everything up again. Especially not on Taylor's birthday, when we're going to have her new friends over."

"That's not selfish. That's loving Taylor and wanting what's best for her."

She put the photo back on the fridge. "Maybe."

"No maybes about it." He studied her for a long moment. "Have you ever thought of seeking custody of her? Taking her in permanently?"

"I think about it all the time. Maybe adopting."

"Is that a possibility? I could put you in contact with a good law firm."

Like she could afford the kind of legal assistance Denny had the funds to retain. From what her aunt had told her, it was top-dollar, go-for-the-throat lawyers who had managed to gain full custody of Denny for Charlotte Gyles.

"I don't know. I mean, I don't want to legally wrestle Annalise's daughter away from her. But I think, for her own good as well as Taylor's, it would be the best thing. I'd be more than willing to bring her home for good."

"Maybe you should talk to your sister the next time she visits. Let her know what you're thinking."

"But what if she takes it wrong?"

"What's to take wrong? Like you said, you're not forcing anything. You're offering. A mother who loves her kid would see your sincerity, the generosity of your proposal."

Tears pricked Lillian's eyes, and she blinked them away. "I would love for that to happen."

"It sounds like a good plan to me."

He stood gazing down at her, a tender reassurance in his eyes. Denny was a good man with a heart of gold. Every time she saw him, talked to him, her day was made a little brighter. She hated to think about him moving on in a few more too-short weeks.

And in that moment, something inside her shifted ever so slightly, and her heart beat faster as their gazes continued to hold. She wet her lips and felt herself sway toward him. Was aware of his hands coming up to gently cup her face.

And then, closing her eyes as he tilted his head and lowered his mouth to hers, she heard the tiniest of sounds behind her.

Chapter Ten

To Denny's disappointed surprise, Lillian turned away at the last moment, and his lips grazed her cheek. Obviously he'd misread the signals in a major way.

She stepped back, firmly pushing him aside. "Taylor! You're done with your bath already?"

"Uh-huh." Standing a few feet away from them, the little girl wrapped in a big plush towel looked from Lillian to him and back again, her eyes dancing. "You were *kissing*."

Not quite, thanks to you, kid. But that had been the plan. Nevertheless, relief flooded him that Lillian hadn't willingly rejected his intention to comfort her.

Ignoring the child's bald-faced declaration, Lillian slipped her arm around her shoulders. "Let's get you dried off, in your jammies and into bed."

She turned Taylor in the direction of the bathroom, but the child peeped around her to look at him, her smile wide. "You were kissing Aunt Lillian."

He held up his hands. "What can I say? She was here."

Lillian cut him a sharp look, but Taylor giggled as she was ushered from the room.

He returned to the dishes, straining in vain to hear what was being said in Lillian's low whispered tones and the soft responses of her niece coming from the bathroom.

He supposed he was going to be in hot water for that almost-kiss. But like he'd told Taylor, she was there. He was there. And Lillian was in need of reassurance. Support. She loved that kid to pieces, and felt helpless to do anything about rescuing her from the sad situation they'd both been forced into by her sister.

Clearly it was getting out of hand, though, when it was causing both of them so much heartache each time the sister put in an appearance—or even when it merely appeared she might, like for this upcoming birthday.

Still, he'd been thinking about kissing Lillian ever since that night in the Hideaway parking lot.

He put the last of the cupcake tins on the dish drainer and reached for a towel to dry them. He was crouched down to a lower cabinet putting them away when Lillian at last returned. She walked straight to the sink and plunged her hands into the cooling water, feeling around for stray items he might have missed.

She released a pent-up breath. "She's so wound up, I don't know if she'll ever get to sleep."

Denny closed the cabinet door and stood, moving to stand behind her. Then wrapping his arms around her, he leaned in to whisper in her ear. "I don't suppose we could pick up where we left off when we were interrupted?"

Quick as a whip, she spun toward him and pressed her hands to his chest, leaving two sopping-wet prints on his blue polo shirt, the glare in her eyes clearly conveying her thoughts: *don't try a stunt like that again, buster.*

He stepped back.

"You might find this whole thing amusing, Denny, but I'm the one having to explain to Taylor what happened between us."

"She didn't seem put off by it—why should you be? Besides, nothing happened."

And didn't he know it. He could still feel Lillian's face cupped in his hands, her whisper-soft breath as he'd angled his mouth over hers.

She grabbed the dish towel off the counter and dried her hands. "And what's Aunt Viola going to think?"

"Who's going to tell her?"

Exasperation flashed in her eyes. "Taylor. Who else?"

"Your aunt likes me. What's the big deal? Nothing happened."

"You should probably go. Aunt Viola will be back any minute, and Taylor will hear her come in and rush out with the news."

"*What* news?"

Had he missed something here? Besides an opportunity to kiss Lillian? Did her flustered state of alarm have anything to do with Todd Samuels? Despite what looked to be the man's blatant efforts to get her attention, she hadn't seemed that interested, although women sometimes played hard to get.

But Denny couldn't be mistaken that when he managed to grab a few minutes with her here and there— like tonight—she seemed to enjoy his company. Nor did she seem opposed to the playful texting flirtation that had developed.

She took him by the arm and steered him toward the door. "Thank you for helping Taylor make cupcakes tonight."

He didn't know how else to categorize the tone of her

voice except as prim. Distant. Had he somehow offended her because he'd tried to kiss her? He couldn't have mis-interpreted the signals to that extreme, could he?

"Look, Lillian, if I've—"

"There's nothing more to be said. Let's put this in the past, please."

She walked him clear to the front door of the inn. "Good night, Denny."

Then she closed and locked the door behind him.

When Denny left, Lillian quickly wrapped up things in the kitchen and quietly welcomed her aunt back home a short time later. Thankfully, Taylor had fallen asleep by then—and the following morning, Aunt Viola slept in long enough for her to get Taylor safely out the door for school.

Even by late afternoon, while settled behind the library's front desk, she still couldn't stop thinking about what had happened between her and Denny.

Or almost happened.

He'd tried to kiss her.

Or actually he *did* kiss her. Sort of. He'd just missed his target with the unexpected arrival of her niece.

Was that why he'd remained in town when he could have left some time ago? As Aunt Vi suspected, did he have an interest in her? She shoved that fleeting hope aside, not willing to go there.

She didn't doubt that her own behavior had led Denny to believe such an attempt was welcomed. She'd let herself all but drown in his sea-blue eyes, then leaned into him as if she couldn't stand on her own two legs. But he had no business trying to kiss her. And she certainly shouldn't have encouraged him to.

All sorts of reasons why kissing wasn't a good idea pounded through her head. First off, they barely knew each other. Plus kisses weren't something she carelessly passed out like candy to neighborhood kids at the holidays. Compounding that, he had no intention of remaining in Hunter Ridge when the inn was finished, so his kissing her amounted to nothing more than toying with her. Passing the time in a little town where there wasn't much else to do, except entertain yourself with a naive local girl.

And yet...her betraying heart had the nerve to relive over and over those tantalizing seconds as his mouth descended, his warm breath hovering over her lips. But wouldn't he hate her if he'd kissed her, then found out she was no more trustworthy than his former fiancée? That she'd ditched her own groom at the altar?

But her most maddening thought?

Now she'd *never* know what it was like to be kissed by Denny Hunter.

"Lillian?"

She jumped at the sound of her manager Jeri's voice.

"Sorry to startle you." Jeri looked around the library almost furtively, her next words a whisper. "Maybe it's not appropriate to tell you this, but I want you to know Reba Clancy did submit an application yesterday."

Despite not being surprised at the news, Lillian's spirits faltered. "Are you telling me this because you think I should withdraw? Save face?"

"I think you're qualified for the position, and I wouldn't have encouraged you to apply if I didn't believe that."

"But that was before we knew for certain Reba had her sights on the job. Her experience runs rings around mine.

We both know, too, that with Cameron's grandmother on the advisory board, the deck is stacked against me."

"Maybe not. She's a savvy businesswoman who has long had to look at difficult issues and weigh them objectively."

"What part of 'she hates my guts' don't you get? This is a woman who wants great-grandchildren, like, yesterday. I was her first real hope that her hard-core bachelor grandson might finally settle down right here in town and start making her dreams come true."

"There are others on the board. She can't steamroller over all of them."

"Don't hold your breath."

"Look, I'm not trying to upset or discourage you by telling you about Reba. I thought you had a right to know."

"Thanks, Jeri. I guess I have a hard decision to make. Throw in the towel now or go down fighting."

"Don't give up, Lillian. Whenever I've applied for jobs, I've always told myself that on any given day I'm the best candidate—that those who are making the decisions can be swayed by God in my favor, no matter how superior I think the competition may be."

"I'll remember that."

When the workday finally ended and she got back to the inn, Todd's crew was finishing up for the day. New insulated windows that fit the age and style of the house had been installed that week, in time for a cold snap that moved in from the north. It was late September, and autumn's prelude to winter was definitely in the air.

When she stepped into the apartment, eager to crash, she halted at the sound of Taylor's giggle—and the sight of Denny seated at the dining table playing Candy Land with her. Her niece was getting a little old for that one, yet she still loved it.

But what was *he* doing here?

"Hey, Lillian," Denny greeted her, and Taylor hopped up from her chair to give her aunt a hug.

"Where's Aunt Vi?"

"In the garden."

Her aunt better not be doing too much bending and kneeling. While modest exercise was good for her, according to her physical therapist, she didn't like the thought of Aunt Viola being out there by herself, unsupervised. What if she got down to pull a weed and couldn't get back up? What if she fell?

Denny stood. "Do you have a few minutes? Maybe we could go for a walk?"

"So you can kiss her again?" Taylor giggled.

"There will be no kissing." Lillian's cheeks warmed as Denny's amused eyes met hers. "Taylor, why don't you see if you can help Aunt Viola?"

"But—"

"Good idea." Denny voiced his support as he placed a hand on Taylor's shoulder. "Your aunt will probably appreciate the company."

Once Taylor left the apartment and they heard her calling to her aunt from outside, Denny motioned to the door. "Shall we?"

She'd rather not. But maybe walking would ease the tension that had clung to her for almost twenty-four hours.

It was still daylight, but the days were getting shorter and shorter, with the sun setting not long after six now. There was a coolness in the air that made her grateful to have slipped into a jacket. Denny had his windbreaker.

"I didn't see your Porsche out front."

"Luke Hunter lent me the blue pickup over there." He nodded to a 4x4 parked just past the inn. "I need to haul stuff to help out Todd's crew, and the sports car didn't fit the bill."

They'd gone but a few blocks down the street in silence when Denny halted. She stopped, too.

He ducked his head slightly to look at her, his words coming softly. "I suppose my trying to kiss you last night means I won't be invited to the birthday party?"

She sighed.

"Are you mad at me because of that, Lillian? Or because you were embarrassed Taylor saw us?" He cut another look at her. "Has she said anything to Viola about it?"

"If she hasn't, she probably is right now. I didn't want to tell her not to say anything to our aunt because that might imply we'd been doing something wrong."

"Nothing wrong at all. But if I misread—"

"You didn't. Nevertheless, it wasn't wise and we both know it."

"That's what I wanted to talk to you about." He glanced around for eavesdroppers, keeping his voice low. "I'm sorry if what I did last night led you on. I was concerned for you and Taylor and what this mess with your sister is doing to you both. I do enjoy your company and, well…"

A pity kiss?

"What was it you told Taylor? You were there, I was there…" Clearly she'd been right. He hadn't given any thought to what a kiss might mean to her until later, then realized that wasn't where he'd intended to go at all. "Don't worry about it. Like I said, it wasn't wise on either of our parts. We're two very different people with vastly different lifestyles, priorities and goals. Anything we'd start now would only end in a bad way for both of us. Taylor, too."

"I'm glad you're not mad. I want us to be friends, if that's okay with you."

An ache growing in her heart promised that it would be a long time before she'd ever think of Denny Hunter as *just* a friend.

"Of course," she said lightly, as if it didn't mean anything one way or another to her. "It's for the best. I want to make my home—Aunt Vi's and Taylor's—in Hunter Ridge. You'll be returning to the world of GylesStyle Inns a few weeks from now. We've both made our choices."

Her words hung in the air between them. What more could be said, anyway? She'd voiced the truth.

And then as the silence stretched, he cleared his throat, a faint smile touching his lips. "While I won't be remaining here, I may not be given the choice of returning to GylesStyle."

"What do you mean?"

"My stepbrother, Vic, was recently promoted to a vice-president position with GylesStyle. One I've worked long and hard for."

"He stole your fiancée *and* your promotion?"

Denny shrugged. "What it boils down to is this—the reason I've stayed in Hunter Ridge for this renovation rather than overseeing it from the Bay Area is because my stepbrother got it in his head that I'm trying to undermine him. And his father—my stepfather and owner of the company—essentially banished me. Blackmailed me, you might say. If I still want to play a part in the company, land a hinted-at-promotion, I have to lie low and stay out of Vic's way for a while."

So his remaining in Hunter Ridge for the renovation had nothing to do with a growing affection for the town—or her.

"But Vic's still floundering, from what I hear," he continued, "and blaming me. My future with GylesStyle Inns is increasingly questionable."

"That is so unfair. That's—"

A few businesses away she glimpsed Cameron's brother sweeping the sidewalk in front of the hardware store. Their eyes met. He grinned, set the broom aside and tucked his fists under his armpits.

Denny's voice was a low growl as he followed her gaze. "I've had it with this kid."

She'd had enough of it, too. Striding ahead, her heels clicking her determination not to shrink from doing what she should have done a long time ago, she planted herself in front of the startled boy, her hands on her hips.

"What is your problem, Randy Gray?"

From the alarmed look in his eyes, he hadn't expected a confrontation. Taking a step back as though fearful she might swing at him, he darted a look around—to see if there was anyone watching who could rescue him?

He took another step back, his face turning red.

"Uh, look, lady, I'm not the one with the problem." He smirked. "You're the one who chickened out. Ditched my brother and left him standing like a goofball in front of the wedding guests. Not me."

Coming up behind Lillian, Denny halted as an invisible fist punched him in the gut.

The boy cut a sympathetic look at him. "Hope you know what you're getting yourself into, *sucker.*"

Again grabbing his broom, the kid ducked inside the hardware store before further words could be exchanged.

Slowly Lillian turned to him, her gaze wary.

She'd dumped some unsuspecting guy on his wedding day? Chicken Man's brother? "That's why he's been strutting around like that every time he sees you?"

She nodded. Barely.

"Why didn't you tell me? Why'd you lead me to believe he was a small-town eccentric I needed to get used to? I was about to grab the kid by the shirt collar and toss him in a chicken coop."

She stepped aside for a passerby. "Could we please not discuss this here?"

"All right." But discuss it they would.

He motioned for them to cross the street and continue their walk. In silence they moved side by side until they rounded a corner to a quiet residential street that led to the church.

"What's the deal, Lillian? Why did you lead me to believe your fiancé was the one to break off your engagement?"

"I never said he was the one to break it off. You jumped to the conclusion that he did."

Had he? "You didn't correct me."

"I know. I'm sorry. I should have told you. I just— You'd shared with me about your breakup. About how your fiancée left you at the altar. I guess…I guess I didn't want you to equate me with her. To judge my situation, my motives, by hers. Maybe withdraw your support of the renovation, and we'd have to cancel Barbie's wedding— and then Aunt Viola would lose her job at the inn, I'd lose a shot at the librarian position, and we'd all have to move to Phoenix, where I could support us."

He shook his head. "Slow down here. I don't see the connection."

"Barbie is my former fiancé's younger sister, and their grandmother is on the library advisory board. Ever since I left her grandson standing at the altar, she hasn't been real fond of me. In fact, my reputation in this town pretty much tanked after that. And if I'm responsible for her granddaughter's wedding day being a disaster? Bye-bye library job for sure."

Denny closed his eyes momentarily, trying to get his head around everything she was firing at him.

"Hold on. You said earlier the guy wanted no part of Taylor or your aunt. Was that true? Or did you make it up to garner my sympathy?"

"It's true. The day before our wedding, Cameron jumped at a job offer back in Boston without consulting me. Informed me that there had been a change in plans, to pack my bags and say farewell to Hunter Ridge."

She took a quick breath, then rushed on. "When I protested that I had a job and responsibilities here, he said I could get a new job, and he'd retain a caregiver for Aunt Viola and foot the bill to place Taylor in a private school. Believe me, I prayed long and hard that night and almost right up until showtime. How could I marry a man like that, Denny?"

He tilted his head to study her, an ache growing in his heart. "You think if you'd have told me the whole story, I'd have thought you *should* have married the guy? That I'd have thought ill of you for having the courage to stand up on your own behalf and the behalf of your aunt and niece at the risk of calling down ridicule on yourself? You don't think a lot of me, do you, Lillian?"

"But I do, Denny. It's that I was scared and so mixed up and—"

"I know we haven't known each other long, but I'd have thought by now that I might have built up some respect in your eyes."

"My mistakes, my poor judgment in this situation, are in no way a reflection on you. Please believe that."

That was going to take some doing.

"I don't know what else to say." Her eyes pleaded for understanding. "Except I'm sorry. I didn't mean to hurt you."

"You didn't." *Liar.* "You just…opened my eyes to reality."

She started to reach for him, but he stepped back. "Let's not beat a dead horse, Lillian. We've got a renovation to finish. Let's focus on business."

But he'd been shaken. Lillian didn't trust him. Didn't respect him. A man could be given the whole world on a silver platter, but if the woman he was coming to care about more than anyone else didn't respect him? Then how could he respect himself?

Realizing there was nothing left to say, he gave her a final searching look, then turned and walked away.

Chapter Eleven

Lillian looked up at the clock. Shouldn't Taylor be home by now? Tonight was the birthday party, and she'd been so excited that Aunt Vi thought she'd probably run all the way home after school. Lillian had taken the afternoon off to put finishing touches on the decorations, blow up balloons and get a pin-the-tail-on-the-donkey game set up.

It had been a rough day, though.

How had things gotten so tangled up with Denny? There were so many misunderstandings on both their parts. If only she hadn't lost her temper with Randy. If only she'd told Denny the whole story of her broken engagement earlier, when she'd had the opportunity.

Friends.

That was what he wanted to be. That was all they could ever be. All she dared to let him be. It was one thing to risk her own heart, to take a chance to win or lose. But she couldn't play games with Taylor's.

Lillian looked at the clock again. Her niece being thirty minutes later than usual made her uneasy. She headed out to the front porch in hopes of spying her coming down the street, when an older-model Toyota pickup pulled up in front of the inn.

Annalise. She looked like a thundercloud, and Taylor, in tears, was seated beside her.

Taylor's mother turned to say something to her, her expression sharp. Irritated. The little girl nodded, then climbed out of the vehicle to race up the porch steps.

Lillian caught her niece's arm. "What's going on?"

Chin quivering and refusing to look at Lillian, she pulled loose and pushed by her and into the inn.

Annalise slowly got out of the pickup and folded her arms. "She's coming with me, Lillian."

Oh, no.

"You don't mean right now, do you? Today's her birthday party."

"I guess you and Lover Boy will have to eat the pretty cupcakes yourselves."

What?

Annalise stepped up on the porch, her expression belligerent and her voice rising. "How *could* you, Lil?"

"What are you talking about?"

"You didn't think Taylor would tell me, did you?"

"Give me a clue here. And hold your voice down." The whole street didn't need to listen in.

"Don't act innocent. I know you're going to try to take her away from me. My own daughter."

"I'm not—"

"Don't lie to me. Taylor wouldn't make something like that up. She says you and your boyfriend are getting married and plan to get a lawyer to gain legal custody of her. Grab her away from me. Adopt her, even."

"I'm not marrying anyone. And I wouldn't—"

"You are a liar in the first degree, Miss Goody Two-shoes. That's one thing Taylor's never done. She's never lied to me, and I don't believe she's lying now."

"Please, Annalise, listen to reason. There's clearly some misunderstanding."

"You can say that again, if you thought you could sneak off and do this behind my back. What were you intending? To slap me with neglect charges? Abandonment? Abuse?"

"I wasn't—"

Annalise stuck her finger in Lillian's face. "Well, you're too late, lady. She's coming with me. Now."

"Annalise, please—"

At that moment, a still-sobbing Taylor stumbled out the front door lugging her suitcase. Aunt Viola was right behind her.

"What's going on?" She looked with alarm from Lillian to her great-great-niece as Taylor dragged the suitcase down the steps.

Annalise shot her a warning look. "You stay out of this, Aunt Vi."

"Don't talk to her in that tone of voice." Lillian kept her voice low, but firm. "You can be rude to me all you want, but I won't allow you to disrespect our aunt."

"It's no secret you've always been her favorite. I imagine she's up to her eyeballs in this plot to snatch away my daughter, too." She looked over her shoulder. "Get in the truck, Taylor."

"Please, Annalise. Don't do this. Not now. It's her birthday..."

The little girl wavered, at long last meeting Lillian's gaze in a silent plea. Without hesitation, Lillian took a step in her direction, but her sister blocked her way and yelled at Taylor. "Drop the suitcase and get in the truck! *Now*."

The little girl quickly obeyed.

"Don't be harsh with her. It's me you're angry with."

"No joke." She moved to the pickup and slung the suitcase in the bed. Jerked open the driver's-side door. "Just so you know, I'm going to find a lawyer of my own and slap a restraining order on *you*, so don't attempt to contact Taylor or raise a legal ruckus. You won't be pulling the wool over my eyes ever again. I won't be messed with."

Annalise climbed into the truck, said something sharp to Taylor, then with a snarl of a smile backed out and headed down the road.

As Lillian stood immobilized with shock, Aunt Viola immediately came to her side and slipped her arm around her waist. "Oh, sweetheart, what happened? Why's she upset?"

Lillian couldn't keep her lower lip from quivering. "I— She thinks I'm trying to take Taylor away from her."

"How did she jump to that conclusion?"

"She says Taylor told her. Told her I was getting married and then I was going to get custody of her."

"Getting married? Why would Taylor tell her that? That's nonsense."

But Taylor had seen that near-kiss between her and Denny. The little girl had clearly been doing her fair share of trying to make a match there. She was obsessed with brides and weddings and happily-ever-afters. Did that almost-kiss imply to her a commitment had been made? Was it wishful thinking on her part that her aunt Lillian and Denny would marry and open their home to her? Then, in a childlike way, she'd unwisely shared that dream with her mother?

"We should call the police," Aunt Vi urged. "Put out an Amber Alert."

"Taylor's in no real danger, and I won't imply to law enforcement that she is." Thankfully, her sister would tear anyone apart who tried to harm her child. "There's never been anything legal drawn up between us, except to give me the right in her absence to make decisions for medical care and school-related issues. Taylor's always come and gone at the whim of her mother, and I chose not to rock the boat for this very reason—that I could lose Taylor entirely."

"Well, there's got to be something we can do."

"Pray." Feeling as if her heart had been ripped in two, Lillian gently pulled away from her aunt. "I'm going for a walk. I can't—I can't talk about this right now. I'll contact the parents, let them know the party's been called off."

"Sweetheart—"

"I'll be fine." She gave Aunt Vi a reassuring smile that she hoped she wouldn't see through. "I need time alone."

Lillian quickly placed the phone calls, providing as little detail as possible. Then woodenly, she walked the winding streets of Hunter Ridge into the early tinges of twilight, heedless of the barking dogs and passing cars.

At long last, she ended up in the deserted community park, children and adults alike having returned home for their evening meal. She sat down on one of the swings, idly pushing herself back and forth in a comforting motion.

Would she ever get the image of Taylor's tear-filled, pleading eyes out of her memory? *Do something. Help me. Don't let Mom take me away.*

But she'd let her niece down.

Please, God, let Taylor understand. Calm Annalise.

Talk sense into her. Please, please make her bring Taylor back to me.

"Lillian?"

She looked up, and in the fading light she saw Denny coming in her direction.

Slowly she stood, acknowledging his presence as he approached. "You heard?"

"Viola told me. Are you okay?"

"I guess. How is *she*?" It had been selfish to leave her aunt alone to grapple with the pain that punctured her own heart.

"She's praying your sister will see the foolishness in what she's done and bring Taylor right back."

"I'm praying that, too."

"I'm sorry, Lillian." He gazed down at her with compassion-filled eyes. "So sorry."

Her chin trembled. "I'm in shock. It happened so fast, it doesn't seem real. I feel as if when I return to the inn, Taylor will come bopping out the door to greet me. To greet *Mister*."

She offered a wobbly smile as her heart wrenched for Denny. He loved Taylor. He'd be hurting, too.

"Oh, Lillian." Without hesitation, he drew her into his arms and she clung to him. Held fast to the arms that sustained her with a strength that surged through her very being. "She'll bring her back. I know she will."

"I'm not sure this time," she whispered against the front of his windbreaker, realizing she'd gone off without a jacket and the air had cooled rapidly once the sun disappeared behind the pine tops. She pressed in closer to his warmth. "I love her and I'm terrified I'll never see her again. That my last memory of her will be of her eyes begging me to *do something*."

Denny's arms tightened around her. "Viola said Taylor told her mother you were getting custody of her. That's what set Annalise off."

Lillian nodded. "I don't know where she got that idea. I've never so much as hinted anything to her about that. Ever."

She felt a groan vibrate his chest. "But you did tell me. Could she have overheard us talking when I asked you about that possibility? Before she walked in on... you know."

Lillian pulled back slightly to look up at him. "Do you think she could have?"

"It's possible."

"But we were just *talking*. Discussing. I was still uncertain if it was something I could pursue. Something I had a right to pursue. Remember?"

"I remember. But maybe she only heard parts of what we said. And then, well, you know—in the excitement, the rest of it may have been forgotten. Or not understood in the first place."

"I feel awful."

"I don't feel much better. I'm the one who broached the topic. I feel responsible for planting the seed that brought about this blowup between you and your sister."

She pressed her hand firmly to his heart. "No. Absolutely do not take this on yourself. If anyone is to blame, it's me."

"How do you figure that?"

"I've too long dreamed of taking Taylor in permanently. I've discussed it with Pastor McCrae and a lawyer. Yet I've never been bold enough to seriously propose it to Annalise. And now it may be too late." Shaking her head, she looked up into his eyes. Then, with a jolt, awareness of how entwined in each other's arms they were shot through her.

Embarrassed, she started to step back. But Denny held her fast, his gaze holding hers captive.

"Don't be afraid, Lillian. I know things seem hopeless right now, but you *will* see Taylor again. I know it."

And then he closed his eyes, lowered his head and tenderly touched his lips to hers.

He heard Lillian's quick intake of breath, but when she didn't pull away he deepened the kiss, longing to comfort her, to assure her that all would be well. Gently cradling her in his arms, he marveled that she was letting him hold her. Was even relaxing into his embrace.

Returning his kiss.

Forget this friends stuff.

The sweetness, the innocence of the moment as time seemed to unfold and slip away, was like nothing he'd ever before experienced. It was giving, not taking. Sharing, not demanding. Her arms slipped around his neck, seeking solace. Offering comfort.

Time stretched and his senses heightened as he drank in the sweet scent of Lillian's hair and the aroma of the surrounding pines. Cool air touched his cheek as twilight deepened. He'd never before felt so alive, and longed for the moment never to end.

But all too soon, Lillian's hands slipped from around his neck, and he reluctantly loosened his hold, although every fiber in him cried out to never let her go. To forever protect her. To somehow make everything right in her world.

She stepped back, looking almost as disoriented as he felt. But he wasn't going to play the gentleman and apologize for that kiss. He had no regrets and hoped she didn't, either.

"Everything is going to be okay," he murmured as he pulled off his windbreaker and slipped it around her shoulders. "I feel it way down deep."

But what he based that on, he had no idea. It wasn't as if he'd ever had a hotline to God. But wherever that conviction came from, he knew he needed to share it with Lillian. Let it give her hope.

She didn't look at him, choosing to stare into the deepening darkness. Was her brain still as befuddled as his was over that kiss? Why did he long for her to acknowledge they'd shared an amazing connection instead of pretending it never happened? He could still feel the electricity in the air. The tension between them.

"I want to believe you, Denny. Oh, how I want to believe you."

"But it hurts like crazy, doesn't it? Taylor being gone is still our reality."

"I hope Annalise doesn't take out her anger with me on Taylor. She was steamed when she left and speaking harshly to her daughter."

"It'll blow over. The whole thing will. The next thing you know, she'll grow tired of parenting once again and come begging you to take Taylor off her hands."

"I pray that's the case. But I don't ever remember her being so angry with me. At least not since we were kids."

They were both silent for a long moment.

"I'd be happy to walk you home." He'd cruised the streets until he'd spotted her, then parked the Porsche nearby. But a drive would be over too quickly, and for some reason he felt a need to remain close to Lillian.

"Thanks. I suppose I should get back to the inn and let Aunt Viola know I'm okay."

"She was worried about you and filled me in when I stopped by to drop off a birthday present for Taylor. A pad of graph paper, a ruler and a mechanical pencil."

"That was sweet of you. So Aunt Vi sent you out like her personal search-and-rescue party?"

"I know how much Taylor means to you. I wanted to be there for you."

"You were there for me all right." He caught a hint of amusement in her tone. Was the kiss lingering in her thoughts as it was in his?

"Anytime."

Her head jerked in his direction. Then she laughed. "Don't tempt me."

He laughed, too, enjoying the sound of their shared mirth, the easing of the tension that followed those more intimate moments.

It wasn't that far to the inn, and they spoke little as they strolled through town. Once there, he declined to come inside, suddenly feeling restless and a need to be alone with his thoughts. His feelings.

But unexpectedly Lillian thrust out her hand. For a shake.

"Friends, Denny?"

What idiot had proposed that as a solution to the attraction sizzling between them?

She was far more sensible than he was. Either that, or an amazing kiss that still left his heart vibrating wasn't as amazing to her as it had been to him, hadn't moved her heart and soul as it had his.

He nodded and grasped her hand, then immediately released it.

"Taylor will be back." He felt as if he needed to leave on a word of hope. "You can count on it."

She gave him an unsteady smile, then slipped inside the inn.

Drawing in a sustaining breath, he retrieved his vehicle, then headed back to the Hideaway, choosing to take it slow down the graveled road, windows down and the cool night air hitting him full in the face.

What had gotten into him tonight?

Lillian's niece had, for all intents and purposes, been abducted, stolen away. No, maybe she wasn't in any kind of immediate danger, but Lillian loved her like a daughter, and her heart was breaking.

Yet he'd taken advantage of her vulnerability tonight. He wasn't proud of himself for that. At least she didn't seem to take offense at the kiss. Wasn't holding it against him.

When he'd stopped by the house to find Lillian gone earlier, Viola explained what triggered Annalise's eruption. Taylor had shared with her that Lillian was going to be married. That the couple would be getting custody of her. Vi suspected she'd overheard her talking to Lillian about Todd and built herself a fantasy, but he knew the miniature matchmaker had another man in mind for Aunt Lillian.

Him.

That was never to be, though. Couldn't be. Not even to make a little girl happy. Maybe in another time and place, under different circumstances. That kiss they'd shared told him there was potential there. Sweeter than sweet, it made him realize what he'd been missing out on in his other relationships. With Corrine in particular, whom he'd come close to marrying.

Lillian was right, though. His future was in the Bay Area at GylesStyle—if he didn't get booted out the door—not in the town the pretty librarian was rooted to. She knew him better than he knew himself.

How would he go about earning a living around here, anyway? Scoop cones at Bealer's Ice Cream Emporium? Serve up hot meals at Rusty's Grill? Paint pretty pictures to sell on consignment at one of the art galleries? He didn't know the first thing about hunting and horses, so he'd be pretty worthless to family members running the Hideaway.

He'd be like a fish out of water here.

And what would he find to do in his spare time besides twiddle his thumbs? The closest thing to a music concert since he'd been here was that country-and-western band that played on Labor Day. And there were zero professional sports teams, unless you drove hours to Phoenix. He lived for a Giants, Warriors or 49ers game. Couldn't get enough of them.

Although he *could* admit he'd gotten a few kicks at Taylor's soccer games.

Instead of heading straight to his cabin, he parked the Porsche in front of the Inn at Hunter's Hideaway, intending to order carryout to cart back to his place. But he'd only shut off the headlights and reached for the door handle when his phone vibrated.

His foolish hopes rose that it might be Lillian saying she'd thought the whole "just friends" thing through and—

But it was Vic. The last person on the planet he wanted to talk to right now. Should he let it go to voice mail? Return it later? Naw, better get this over with.

"Yo, Vic."

"Den, do you have a minute?"

"A few."

"Hey, I know since I stepped into the VP slot we haven't had time to sit down and discuss your role in the company. So I wanted to touch base with you about an opening that's recently come up. Something I think you'd be a good fit for."

Denny's spirits rose. He'd stayed out of Vic's way for over a month, hadn't interfered even when Craig had been let go. Was this the opportunity with the company that Elden Gyles had alluded to, should Denny keep out of the limelight?

"What do you have?"

"It won't be announced until tomorrow, but you may have heard Barry Swoffard resigned this afternoon?"

A muscle in Denny's neck tightened. Barry had managed the Midwest region from Kansas City for almost a decade—one of the many regions under Denny's oversight. No way would Barry willingly resign. He loved his job. Had he been another victim of Vic's housecleaning?

"No, I hadn't heard that. That's unexpected. What happened?" Why hadn't Barry called him?

"He wants to spread his wings elsewhere. So does that spot interest you?"

That was what Vic had in mind for *him*? A demotion? Expulsion from the San Francisco office altogether? That wasn't what Denny envisioned the dangled carrot to be when he'd buckled under Elden Gyles's mandate to renovate his mother's inn and lie low.

"There's plenty of opportunity in the Midwest region that hasn't been tapped," Vic continued. "We need fresh blood in that role. Imagination. Creativity. Someone who knows the industry. In other words, you."

Did Vic think he was selling this opportunity to him? That Denny couldn't see right through what was really going on? He drew a breath, ready to explode and deliver his honest opinion. He and Vic had been heading for a showdown since the beginning of the year. It was about time Vic got the earful he deserved.

Don't burn your bridges yet.

"Den? You still there?"

"Just thinking." The tension inexplicably ebbed out of him as his mind raced, exploring his options. Something had checked him, and he didn't want to blindly push ahead without knowing what it meant, or do something he might later come to regret. "If it's okay with you, I have a few more weeks here on that personal project my mother and Elden have me working on. I can get back with you then. Maybe with a few innovative ideas for the Midwest region."

"Oh?" Obviously Denny's response wasn't what he'd expected. No doubt he'd hoped his younger stepbrother's objections would be the needed excuse to deliver a "my way or the highway" speech and fire him on the spot like he'd done Craig and probably Barry. Would such a move have Elden's blessing? Was the proud papa giving his egotistical son free rein? Denny sure wouldn't go whining to Elden about this latest turn of events.

"Well, that would be great," Vic finished lamely. "Get in touch with me when you're ready."

"Will do. And, Vic?"

"Yeah?"

Denny couldn't help but smile. "Congratulations on your upcoming nuptials. Give Corrine my best."

Chapter Twelve

To Lillian's relief, Denny had hung in there on the Pine-wood Inn—and for the next several weeks he, Todd's crew, and assorted plumbers, electricians and stone-masons pushed ahead on the inn. They were slightly ahead of schedule, enabling the inspectors to do their business almost a week before the team's targeted dead-line—Barbie's October wedding.

Now they awaited word on whether or not the inspection had been approved and they could finish up. But in past weeks, the days hadn't been without setbacks—delayed or damaged deliveries, a death in the family of one of Todd's crew, which took her away from the project. Installation of bathroom fixtures taking longer than expected. A countertop that had been cut wrong and had to be returned for a trim.

And no word from Annalise. Not so much as a post-card to let her and Aunt Viola know where they were. That they were okay.

She'd held tightly to Denny's adamant insistence that Annalise would again tire of parenthood and seek out her big sister. But what if she'd found someone else to entrust her daughter to?

Was Taylor eating right? Getting enough sleep? Had she been enrolled in school? Her teacher in Hunter Ridge had been devastated to lose her so early in the year. After the first week following her departure, Lillian had put away the birthday-party decorations. But wrapped packages—from her, Aunt Vi and Denny—still lay on the rollaway bed Taylor slept on in Lillian's room. Her heartfelt prayers flowed constantly to a God who cared.

"You doing okay?" On his way to the storage room to drop off another big box of new bath towels, Denny stopped in the remodeled kitchen, where Lillian was putting shelf liner in the cabinets. Yes, it was premature, but it gave her something to do to occupy her mind.

"Pretty good." As well as could be expected, she supposed, when every time she heard a child giggle or glimpsed a photo of Taylor on the fridge, her stomach knotted.

Denny had kept pretty much to himself since that kiss in the park that she still relived over and over, but he did check in with her on occasion to offer a word of encouragement. She could tell Taylor was on his mind, too.

"I know you're holding your breath waiting for word on the librarian position." He shifted the oversize box in his arms. "They're taking their sweet time. Keeping you in limbo."

"Maybe Cameron's grandmother is holding the advisory board hostage until they come around to see things her way."

"You thought the interview went well, though, right?"

"It seemed to. Mrs. Gray was all business—at least, no personal potshots. She probably saved those for behind the scenes."

He placed the box on the floor and leaned back against the new kitchen island. Folded his arms.

"Not that it's my business...and feel free to tell me to bug off. But how are you going to hold down a full-time librarian position and manage the inn, too?"

"Aunt Vi is the inn's manager, not me."

"I know you'd like me to believe that, Lillian, but I'm not swallowing it. In August I had my doubts, but you reassured me, and my mother certainly wanted to believe it. But that's not going to happen, is it?"

"She's making wonderful headway. If you could have seen her earlier this year—"

"But it's been a good nine months since her fall. Not only do I have two eyes in my head, but I know enough about broken hips to know that only a fraction of those who suffer one make anything close to a full comeback. So I'm asking you again. How do you intend to hold down the library position and manage the inn?"

Lillian put down the shelf liner. "You're not thinking of telling your mother not to renew Aunt Vi's contract, are you? Of advising her to hire someone else to manage the Pinewood?"

"You still haven't answered my question."

"I can do it, Denny."

"How?"

"Well, I've *been* doing it, haven't I?"

"While working at the library only part-time."

"There's not that big of a difference between thirty and forty hours a week. I won't be working on weekends, which is when the inn will be its busiest. In the winter months, when it's not right around the holidays, the place will probably be close to empty. Work here will be fairly seasonal. And Aunt Vi can still keep the books, fix breakfast and make people feel at home."

"Who will tend her garden that keeps people booking events?"

"I will. I enjoy doing that."

"In all your spare time."

He pushed off from the island and lifted the box again. "I'm not saying it can't be done, Lillian—or that you won't give it all you've got. But I am concerned. My mother invested a great deal of money in renovating this place. I'd hate to see it bring no more return on her investment now than it has since she first acquired it from my dad."

He deposited the box in the storage room, then headed back toward the front of the inn. She followed, determined to continue their conversation—then halted when she saw her aunt coming through the front door. Saw her through Denny's eyes. The limp. The balance issues. The sometimes-obvious fatigue.

But Lillian also saw the resilience, the sparkle in her eyes that said the game wasn't over yet. Not by a long shot.

And Lillian wasn't about to let Denny call a halt to it prematurely.

"How was the ladies' tea, Aunt Vi?"

"Delightful. I wish you could come sometime."

"I—"

She heard Denny's phone vibrate. He pulled it out and held it to his ear.

"I'd love to go sometime, Aunt Vi. Maybe when I can—"

Denny held up his hand for silence as he listened intently. His bright-eyed gaze swept over her and her aunt.

"Yeah, yeah, they're both right here beside me waiting to hear the inspection verdict."

Aunt Vi held up her hands, fingers crossed, as she exchanged an anxious look with Lillian.

"Sure. Sure." Denny nodded, and then his brows lowered. "I see. Sorry to hear that, Todd. Know you are, too."

Looking down at the floor, avoiding their anxious gazes, he listened to what must be a rambling discourse on Todd's end.

Lillian took her aunt's hand as the conversation wrapped up. From what they could hear, things didn't sound good.

"Appreciate the call, Todd."

Still not looking at them, Denny slipped the phone into his pocket. "Well, ladies, I'm afraid I have some news to report."

When he was certain he could keep a straight face, Denny looked at Lillian and Viola, who were both staring at him, hope fading from their eyes.

Were he and Todd troublemakers or what?

"I have to report—" unable to keep them going any longer, he grinned "—that the inn passed inspection with flying colors!"

"*What?* You, you—" Lillian doubled up her fist like she was going to sock him. He deserved it. Todd, too. "You rat! How can you guys do that to us?"

"So it's a go?" Vi wasn't taking any chances that she'd misunderstood.

"It's a go. A few minor things the inspectors would like us to do, but they've signed off and we're set to move toward our deadline."

Viola clapped. "In time for Barbie's wedding and reception."

"Woo-hoo!" Lillian high-fived her aunt. "And now there will be a room fit for a queen if she and her two bridesmaids want to dress here before the ceremony."

"That's the plan, anyway," he warned, feeling that he had to use caution despite the relief flowing through him. As much as he'd enjoyed the work, he hadn't realized how on edge this thing had made him. "The interior walls and ceilings may have been textured, but they still need to be painted and window treatments hung. And after that the new furnishings have to be brought in from the local warehouse where they've been stored. But we have five days before the wedding to do as much of it as we can, and the painters are coming in tomorrow. It will be tight and we may burn the midnight oil, but I think we'll get 'er done."

"We will," both women said in unison. Then hugged each other.

More than anything in the world, he wanted to pick Lillian up, swing her around and plant a kiss on her now-smiling mouth. But he restrained himself. "Friends" shouldn't get carried away.

"Would you ladies do me the honor of joining me for dinner tonight? In hopes of good news today, I reserved a table at the Inn at Hunter's Hideaway."

Both women nodded their agreement, and the evening ended on an especially happy note as they celebrated their weeks of hard work. But more work was yet to come, and they were up early the next morning to get things ready for the painters who were scheduled to arrive at seven.

Eight o'clock rolled by. Then nine. No painters.

"My phone calls go to voice mail." Denny looked to Lillian, who was standing by her aunt, peering out the front window.

"Not good," she responded with a worried look.

"It's odd. They were prompt on the days they were texturing and priming the walls."

"I wonder if they got their days mixed up. Did you call them yesterday to confirm?"

"Maybe I should have. But I talked to them Friday and everything was set."

"I wonder if—"

His phone vibrated, and he whipped it out. "Maybe this is them."

But he shook his head at Lillian when Todd greeted him.

"You may have already heard, but your painters were coming back from a job in Show Low late last night. Hit an elk. Rolled their van."

"Are they okay?"

"Hospitalized. Pretty banged up. Broken bones. I think Penny and Dee Dee may be released this afternoon or sometime tomorrow. No word on Mia. But none of them are in any shape to start that job."

Without the place painted, they couldn't do a final cleanup and bring in the furnishings and other decorative materials.

"Can you round up anyone else? Someone who would do a good job, I mean?"

"I called around before I called you, and so far nothing's panning out. A few teams would like the job, but won't be available until after the first of next month."

After the wedding.

"If you'd keep your ears open for a replacement, we'd appreciate it. We don't have many days left to pull this off, and this place is big. It can't be painted in an afternoon."

"Don't I know it. I'll keep you posted."

"Thanks." The call concluded and Denny turned to Lillian and Viola. "Know a good florist in Show Low?"

"What happened to our painters?"

"Hit an elk last night."

"Bull elk?" Viola's eyes widened. "Those things can weigh up to a thousand pounds or more."

"Don't know, but it rolled them. I guess they're in pretty bad shape. One's worse than the other two."

Vi moved off in the direction of the apartment. "I'll get the number of the florist I use."

Lillian turned desperate eyes on him. "So what are we going to do now?"

He hitched a brow. "How are you with a paint roller?"

"I hope you're not serious. Getting this place painted in time to allow us to get the furnishings in before the wedding was going to be a stretch even for those three pros."

"I won't argue that. I was thinking it would be optimistic to get the downstairs done. But now…" He shook his head.

"But now what?" a booming voice called from the open doorway.

What was his dad doing here? "We've run into a snag with our painters. It doesn't look like we're going to meet our deadline."

And if they didn't meet the deadline, Lillian would risk getting even further on the bad side of her former fiancé's grandmother, and he'd be stuck here for who knew how long.

His dad joined them in the parlor. "I can swing a brush with the best of 'em."

"Thanks, but we're weighing our options right now." Which weren't many. "What brings you here?"

"I haven't been inside this building for thirty years, so thought I'd stop in and look around." His dad cut a look at Lillian, then jerked his head in Denny's direction. "You probably know that his mother—"

"Dad."

Doug Hunter laughed, then motioned to Lillian. "Actually I thought I'd come in and get a closer look at the young lady who seems to be occupying all my son's time. He's hardly said boo to his old man since he got to town."

Color tinged Lillian's cheeks when she met Denny's apologetic gaze. "It's the inn renovation, Mr. Hunter, that's keeping him busy."

"You think so? Haven't looked in the mirror lately, have you? And call me Doug."

"Dad."

"Oh, stop being such a killjoy. I'm teasing your pretty lady here. I'm sure she knows how to take ribbing in the right spirit of things. Don't ya?"

"I do my best."

"You've had plenty of practice, I imagine, what with running off on your last groom." He winked at her. "Denny's been dumped once, so I'm counting on you to stick with this one."

"Dad. I think it's time for you to go."

He chuckled as he raised his hands. "No harm intended. Don't go running me off just yet. It sounds as if you're going to need help around here."

"I appreciate the offer. But like I said, we're weighing options."

"That's my son all right. He thinks too much when the situation calls for action." Doug again winked at Lillian. "That's probably why he isn't married yet."

Her eyes met Denny's again, and he caught a flash of

amusement. Glad she was finding his father funny. He sure wasn't.

Vi returned with the florist's phone number and struck up a conversation with his dad, which enabled Lillian to slip from the room. He followed her to the kitchen.

"I apologize for my dad's behavior. He sometimes gets carried away. And *please* don't say anything tacky like I'm just like him."

"You're nothing like him, I can assure you."

Denny swiped at his brow and gave her a grin.

"So what are we going to do, Denny? What are these options you seem to think we have?"

"To be honest? That talk was solely for the benefit of Dad. If he thought I didn't have a clue, he'd think that was the signal for him to step in and take over. Which, believe me, is not something we want to have happen." Denny ran his hand roughly through his hair, suddenly weary. "Todd's trying to round up replacement painters, so I guess we sit tight and hope he can pull some out of the woodwork by tomorrow."

"Because if he doesn't…"

"There's no reason the garden wedding and reception can't proceed as planned. It doesn't have to be canceled. We passed inspection. The caterers can take over the kitchen, and for the most part, things are pretty well cleaned up. Your grandmother of the bride shouldn't have anything to whine about."

"But there's scaffolding all over the back where the painters were doing trim. And stupid me, when things were coming along so well, I promised the bride a guest room for her and her bridesmaids to get ready in. But there's no furniture. Not even window treatments for privacy."

"We can get the scaffolding taken down, and Barbie can

make do with folding chairs and a sheet tacked up at the window. If this glitch is the worst thing that happens to her in her married life, she should consider herself well off."

Lillian frowned. Something else was bothering her.

"What am I missing here?"

"Cameron."

She was thinking about her former fiancé? "What about him?"

"He had some rude things to say about the inn and my dreams for it when he was trying to convince me to go to Boston and retain a caregiver for Aunt Vi."

Ah. "You think he'll be coming to the wedding."

She nodded. "I know it's dumb, but I wanted everything to be done. Perfect."

He wanted it to be perfect for her, too.

"I wish I could promise it will be. But realistically, we may not get painters in here for several weeks—either the ones who started the project or a replacement team. Then the furnishings after that."

"Like I said, it was a stupid hope in the first place."

"No hope is stupid." And no doubt she'd planned to be dressed to the nines, hair and makeup flawless, and make the guy eat his heart out when he saw the Pinewood Inn's beautiful hostess.

"We'll figure something out. Don't you worry."

But he'd told her not to worry about Taylor, too, and that Annalise would be carting her back home in no time. That hadn't happened, either.

He'd never been much into praying. But for Lillian, this might be a good time for him to start.

Lillian awoke the next morning earlier than usual, the room still dark except for a thin line of light coming from under the bedroom door. But when she turned on her bedside lamp and her eyes alighted on Taylor's birthday presents atop the empty bed across the room, her already gloomy thoughts darkened. She nevertheless managed a whispered prayer for her niece and sister before becoming conscious of the sounds that had roused her from her sleep.

Voices. Male and female. Laughter.

It wasn't yet 6:00 a.m.

Scrambling to grab her robe, she slipped it on, then stepped into the main room of the apartment. The door was open to the inn's hallway, the voices louder now, sounding like a small army had taken up residence.

A robed Aunt Vi, her eyes twinkling, came through the door and, spying her, motioned her forward. "Come, Lillian. I didn't think you'd ever wake up. You can't miss this."

She stepped into the hallway with her aunt, and they moved to the parlor, which was packed with people in work clothes milling about, boxes of doughnuts being passed among them.

Denny's dad and uncle Dave. His aunt Elaine and grandma Jo. His Hunter half siblings, cousins and all their spouses. Sawyer Banks and his new bride, Tori, too. Cash Herrera. So many church members she recognized spilling out onto the lit front porch. In the far corner was a smiling Sharon Dixon Diaz, owner of Dix's Woodland Warehouse over in Canyon Springs. At her side was her husband, Bill, along with members of their extended family. Kara and Trey. Joe and Meg. Abby and Brett.

And there, smack in the middle of the hubbub, was Denny.

Bewildered, she cupped her hands to her mouth and yelled, "What's going on?"

He immediately made his way over to her, looking as shell-shocked as she felt. "I was rolled out of bed at five o'clock by Dad and told to get myself over to the inn pronto. That there was work to be done."

"You mean—?"

"He means that even though Denny's done his best to evade us while he's been here, he's still a Hunter." A grinning Pastor McCrae slipped his arm around his wife, Jodi. "So it's Hunter family and friends to the rescue. Point us to the paint cans and roller brushes and we'll make this thing happen."

Her astonished gaze collided with Denny's. "Is this for real?"

"Sure looks like it. But now I have to restore order and come up with a workable plan. Maybe split people into shifts. First coat today, second tomorrow. Penny, our painter, is here. With broken ribs too sore to paint, but she'll supervise and provide instruction so this gets done right."

Still overwhelmed, Lillian looked around at the crowd. "Some of these people I recognize as being from out of town, so make sure to get them assigned to something today. We don't want them to have to make a return trip."

He nodded. "Stick close and help me sort this out, okay?"

"I will. But let me get dressed first. Do something with this crazy hair."

"You look fabulous to me, even with bedhead and a fuzzy robe. So don't take long. Let's get this thing organized and hit the ground running."

The next three days were a whirlwind of activity,

with Penny roaming both inside and out, giving technique demonstrations and tips to ensure drop cloths were draped strategically and quality work was being done. During breaks Denny provided enough sandwiches and pizzas to keep the hungry mob filled, and limitless energy and high spirits seemed to bounce off the walls of the inn.

"I still can't believe these people volunteered to help us." Denny shook his head in wonder at the lunchtime crowd gathered around tables in the garden. "Most of these people I don't even know. They don't know *me*."

"But they do know my aunt and me—and they want to get to know you. Your family turned out, too. I've never seen so many Hunters together at one time, except at big celebrations."

Denny shook his head again. "That's especially mind-boggling because as the son of Charlotte Gyles, they don't even *like* me."

"What do you mean? Of course they like you, or they would have quietly gone about their own business. They all have better things to do than take time off from work and get covered with paint. You heard Garrett—you're a Hunter. That counts for something in their eyes."

"I suppose." He didn't look convinced. "But what about the others who aren't related to me? What's in it for them?"

She laughed and linked her arm through his. "This is one of the perks of a small town, Denny. Of having a church family. Now you know why I desperately want to call Hunter Ridge my home."

His gaze met hers and held, still uncomprehending perhaps, but he nodded thoughtfully.

Longing to reach out to him and convince him of his

worth, she could no longer deny that somewhere in the past weeks she'd come to love him. For too long she'd let regret of the past and fear of the future steal her joy, hold her back. Was she now truly willing to trust God and risk her heart?

But she'd fallen for someone who wanted to be *just friends*. Someone who, like her niece, feared stepping out and surrendering his heart to those who loved him.

But even if he could somehow overcome that, would Hunter Ridge hold him for a lifetime? Could she? How long would it be until, like her former fiancé, he felt smothered, trapped in the tiny town, and returned to life in a metropolis teeming with like-minded people and what he perceived as limitless opportunities?

Could she bring herself to leave the town that meant so much to her and follow him wherever his life might lead if it meant uprooting Aunt Viola—and, God willing, Taylor—to follow her heart?

Lord, what am I to do?

If only Taylor would return soon.

And Denny would change his mind about being just friends.

Chapter Thirteen

With the painting completed and downstairs furnishings brought in the day of the wedding rehearsal, the hours before Barbie Gray's long-awaited afternoon were a flurry of activity. To Denny's relief, the day was warm and sunny, perfect for an outdoor wedding.

While Lillian oversaw the staging of the garden, with pristine white folding chairs arranged around the front of the gazebo, and assisted the caterers with waist-high cocktail-type tables for the reception, her aunt helped them set up in the kitchen.

Denny had kept himself out of the way for the most part, focusing on getting the window treatments up in the front parlor and other downstairs rooms. They wouldn't be reopening for guest bookings until the week of Thanksgiving, so there was plenty of time to furnish and decorate the upstairs, to ensure they were cleared to again receive paying overnight visitors. But at least the downstairs would be showcase-perfect for the bride—and Lillian.

"You're coming right along here," Viola said from the doorway, approval evident in her voice.

"Wrapping it up. Downstairs, anyway." He stepped down from the ladder. "And astonishingly, with an hour to spare before the bride and her entourage are scheduled to put in an appearance."

Viola gazed happily around the room. "Who would have thought the Pinewood could look like this in such a short time?"

"Hard work and teamwork."

"Thank you, Denny, for so much." She crossed the room to give him a hug. "Not just the renovation, but for convincing your mother we can do this."

That still remained to be seen. A now-five-bedroom inn with a lovely garden setting might not ever be a true moneymaker. But his mother was willing to take that chance.

"It's been my pleasure." And despite its ups and downs, it *had*, for the most part, been a pleasure. Working with Todd's team, enjoying that amazing time when the Hunters and friends had jumped in to help out and, most of all, spending time with Viola and Lillian. And his precious Taylor.

He hated to see that come to an end.

"I guess I should say my goodbyes now, before wedding guests start arriving."

"Goodbyes?" Viola's smile crumpled. "You're leaving?"

"As soon as I pick up my stuff from the Hideaway. It's time to get back to my real life." He'd decided to take his stepbrother up on the Midwest position. While a demotion, he liked the thought of confounding Vic, leaving him guessing as to his little brother's motives, and was determined to make a go of it while staying plugged into the heart of GylesStyle Inns.

"Does Lillian know?"

"Does Lillian know what?" Lillian echoed.

He looked in the direction of her voice, and his breath caught. Dressed in a forest green, just-above-the-knee sheath dress with a matching fitted jacket and black heels, she was a vision.

He blinked. "Wow."

Viola beamed. "She cleans up nice, doesn't she, Denny?"

"I'll say. Not that she's ever looked less than sharp, but today she's a knockout."

He couldn't take his eyes off her. Was he out of his mind to be hitting the road? For insisting they keep their relationship as friends only? He could find a job around here someplace, right? Washing cars. Raking yards. Busing tables and mucking out stalls at the Hideaway, as his dad had made him do that summer he'd visited here when he was twelve years old.

But then again, it would only be a matter of time, wouldn't it, until Lillian figured out what Corrine hadn't— or at least hadn't acted on—until their wedding day. That he wasn't that much of a catch in the long run.

"Denny's leaving." Viola gave her niece a look he wasn't sure how to interpret. "This afternoon."

With startled eyes, Lillian tipped her head to look at him over the top of her glasses, a familiar mannerism he'd always treasure. "So soon?"

Viola slipped past Lillian, patting her on the arm. "I need to change clothes, too. Although I doubt I'll leave Denny's mouth hanging open like you did."

Lillian's cheeks pinkened.

"You do look amazing," he acknowledged when Viola left the room.

"Thank you." She offered a slight smile. "But you're leaving *today*?"

"You knew I'd only be here a short while. The time's flown. Now I need to get back to where I belong."

But his heart would always be here. With Lillian.

"So you're getting that promotion your stepfather promised if you completed this project and kept your distance from the main office during your stepbrother's adjustment period?"

"Actually...no." He hated admitting he was being shoved aside, deliberately overlooked. But he'd do his best to turn it around, make it work, garner his stepbrother's grudging respect if it was the last thing he ever did. "Vic's transferring me to the Midwest to oversee our operations there. I need to wrap things up in the Bay Area office and get on with it. Pay my dues and hope for the best."

"Midwest operations. But isn't that—?"

"Correct. For all intents and purposes, a demotion."

Her eyes filled with understanding. "I'm sorry, Denny. You did everything you were asked."

"To the best of my ability."

"I don't think I like your family."

"Sometimes I don't, either. But for the time being, I need to roll with the punches. Not give Vic the satisfaction of being free of me just yet—which I believe was his intention with this transfer. He wanted me to balk so he could fire me outright. I think it threw him in a major way when I didn't."

She sighed. "It's all such a game."

"It's one I've played for many years. Win some, lose some. I'm not done winning just yet."

"I admire that about you."

"Being stubborn?"

"Never giving up."

But he'd given up on Lillian, hadn't he? Too scared to risk her discovering the man others had come to know—and rejected.

She moved to stand by him and took hold of his upper arm. Staring down at her hand—the same soft, gentle hand that reached out to care for her aunt, to comfort Taylor, to touch his face that night in the dark Hideaway parking lot—he didn't want to hear what she had to say. It was time to move on.

As if sensing his desire to pull away, her grip tightened, and he reluctantly met her gaze. Those beautiful eyes.

"Denny," she said quietly, "believe me when I say I respect you more than any other man I've ever known. I admire so much about you, about who you are. Your accomplishments. The way you've overcome the challenges life has thrown at you. I have high regard for your integrity and am in awe of your diverse talents and capabilities. My heart tugs every time I see the sensitive way you interact with Aunt Viola—and our dear little Taylor. And, too, when I see how this past week you've gradually made room in your heart for your Hunter family, and you're attempting to build a relationship with your long-estranged father."

Denny's hungering heart swelled at her words, the admiration in her eyes and the approval in her tone. He drank it in, like a man thirsting in the desert who'd stumbled on an oasis, a pool of clear, cold water.

But then reality hit and he chuckled. "Why is it I hear a 'but' coming?"

"Because it is." The glow in her eyes dimmed. "I respect you in boundless ways, Denny Hunter. But I have to confess that, sadly, you put more stock in what other people think of you than what God thinks of you. Desiring to earn the respect of others is admirable. But without love…something is missing."

He looked away. She wasn't telling him anything he wasn't aware of. "As I shared from my former fiancée's wedding-day text message, I'm not an easy man to love. Even God has His work cut out for Him there."

She drew him back to look at her, her eyes wide with disbelief. "I disagree. You're an easy man to love—and in a very short time, I've come to care deeply for you."

His heart stilled. Was she implying she'd come to care for him as more than a friend? No, she was speaking *as* a friend. Wasn't that what he'd told her he wanted? All he could offer her?

"But like my niece," she continued softly, "you slam the door when you sense someone is getting too close. Someone who might see through the protective layers you've built around your heart. Who might see into the core of who you are. You fear if you let them in longer than a fleeting moment, they'll reject you. And that will hurt. So you hold everyone at arm's length—including, most sadly of all, the God who loves you."

Denny stiffened. He had to get out of here. Her words were smothering him. Strangling him. Confusing him.

He grunted. "Nice theory you have there."

"There's truth in it."

Maybe there was. Maybe there wasn't. But he'd known since he was a boy that love was undependable, ephemeral, doled out to those who deserved it. Who were, by their very nature, *lovable*.

But *respect*? Respect could be earned if you worked

hard enough at it. He knew that for a fact. He'd spent a lifetime proving it.

He glanced out the front window to the porch, where Lillian had transformed it for Barbie Gray's afternoon wedding with flowers and fluttering ribbons. "Thanks for the pep talk, but I don't want to keep you any longer. You have a wedding to put on and I've got to get going. If I start now, I can get to San Francisco in the wee hours of the morning."

"You really are leaving."

"The inn's finished. Nothing to keep me here."

He caught the flinch in her eyes. She drew a breath. "Well, then, give me a hug."

He opened his arms and she stepped into them as if she belonged, and for a long moment he held her pressed to his heart. Drank in the sweet scent of her. He hated this "just friends" stuff. But their relationship was never meant to be anything more. Even if things would have gone in another direction, he could never ask her to pull up roots that had grown deep in Hunter Ridge. This was her home.

The home of her heart.

He couldn't compete with that.

The arms that wrapped around his waist gave him a hard, final squeeze. Then she stepped back.

"Take good care of yourself, Denny."

"You, too. Let me know when Taylor returns."

"I will."

And then, his heart aching, he left the inn, pulling the door soundly shut behind him.

In the car he turned up the stereo to drown out his turbulent thoughts. But channel after channel flooded the airwaves with a mournful wail of long-lost love. No wonder he used to hate country and western. He switched it off, only to drown in the silence. It seemed like a long drive back to the Hideaway, where he packed up his things and loaded the car.

He had a box to leave at the Hideaway's front desk for pickup—something for Lillian. But before he could see to that, he found himself impulsively turning down the graveled lane to his dad's place on the Hunter property.

When he knocked, Vickie came to the door. Her tone was welcoming, but her eyes were curious. "Come in, Denny."

"Thanks." He stepped into the living room. "I can't stay long."

Maybe he shouldn't have come at all. Just texted his goodbyes once he hit the city limits.

"Why can't you stay long?" Dad demanded from where he'd stretched out in his recliner, watching TV. "You have time for everybody but your old man."

He irritably grabbed the remote and shut off the TV as Vickie motioned for Denny to sit down. He did. Then she silently left the room.

"I wanted to let you know I'm heading to the Bay Area, then taking a transfer to the Midwest. I don't know when I'll be back this way."

Maybe never.

His dad hit the recliner release and sat up straight, his expression perplexed. "You're leaving? But I thought you and Lillian—"

Denny waved his dad off. He didn't want to talk about Lillian. "That's not working out."

"What do you mean?" Dad leaned forward. "I had a front-row seat this past week to how that gal brightens up like a light bulb when you walk into the room. I could say the same about you when she smiles in your direction."

"Yeah, well, Aunt Elaine says you and Mother started out that way, too. So it's better to recognize now that there's no future for us. Before we sign on the dotted line. Before kids get thrown into the mix."

But Taylor had stolen his heart weeks ago. Would he ever see her again?

A heavy silence filled the room, and Denny longed for a rewind to drive on past the turnoff to his dad's place and hit the road.

His father clasped his hands together, his expression earnest. Troubled. "Char and I—we did you wrong, Denny."

"That's water under the bridge." He didn't have it in him to listen to his father rail about the long-dead relationship.

Dad shook his head. "I said *both* of us did you wrong, Denny. Not just your mother. We were young and selfish and didn't heed the counsel of those older and wiser— like Viola and your grandma Jo. Looking back, knowing what I now know having been married to Vickie for nearing three decades, I realize we could have made it work if we'd have stopped thinking solely of ourselves. Stopped looking at what we wanted to get out of the relationship rather than what we could give to it. We owe you an apology."

Denny shifted uncomfortably, unaccustomed to confessions of wrongdoing coming from his father.

"It's better to let things between Lillian and me die a natural death. Eventually she'd recognize what *you* knew when I was a kid—that I'm not easy to love."

"I never thought that."

"You said it."

"When?"

It was as clear in Denny's mind as if it were yesterday. "You'd taken me fishing the last full day I was here, remember? In that old rattletrap truck of yours. You'd packed us lunches, let me use your best rod and reel and everything. And when we were packing up our gear at the end of the day, that's when you told me, 'Son, you're not an easy kid to love.'"

Dad shook his head. "You misunderstood."

"How?"

He may have been a kid, but he did understand English. And he wasn't stupid.

"I wasn't saying I didn't love you, that you weren't worthy of being loved. That I thought you were *unlovable*." Compassion flickered through his father's eyes, an expression Denny wasn't accustomed to seeing there. "I was referring to the fact that you didn't make it easy on anyone who tried to love you."

"But—"

Dad stood to look down at him.

"You were always throwing up barriers. Backing away. Just as you'd done that day we'd gone fishing and I tried to put my arm around your shoulders." He mimed the action. "You shook me off like you didn't want any part of that. Any part of *me*."

Dad shook his head, pain of the memory clearly reflected in the gaze he centered on Denny. "I can't tell you how many times I tried the week you were here to break down the walls you'd built, but you'd have none of it. So I didn't force the issue when you told your mother you never wanted to visit me again."

Denny stared at his father—searching his eyes, seeking the truth. *No way.* No way had he misunderstood what his dad had said. It had fit with everything he'd ever known. His mother often saying his dad didn't have time to come visit him. His mother and stepfather sending him off to a private out-of-state school so they didn't have to deal with him, their *unlovable* kid.

"Den," Dad said gently, "you'd built walls so high, a mountain climber couldn't have scaled them. That's why I was tickled to death to see that little runaway bride somehow managing to dig her way under."

Denny's brain struggled to make sense of what his father was saying. The jumbled pieces slowly came together.

Had Lillian been right about him?

"Don't let her slip away from you, son. You'll regret it for the rest of your life."

Chapter Fourteen

She'd taken a stand. Trusted God.

And lost Denny.

He couldn't see beyond the fortifications he'd constructed around his heart, choosing instead to retreat into what must be a lonely self-confinement. Isolating himself from God. From others.

From her.

What could she have said or done differently that would have convinced him, opened his eyes, his heart?

She'd lain awake the past several nights going over everything they'd both said that last day. She'd garnered the courage to tell him how deeply she cared for him, yet that didn't so much as chip his self-protective armor. So determined to remain *just friends*, he'd flicked off her confession as carelessly as if it had been a ladybug on his sleeve.

That hurt. And when he said the inn was finished and there was nothing to keep him here?

She couldn't *make* him love her, though. Not the way she wanted to be loved. The way she loved *him*.

Savagely she clipped back the now-fading chrysanthemums. Barbie's wedding had been the last garden event of the season—beautiful in every way. Lillian even had time to speak to Cameron in private to apologize. He'd admitted he'd provoked her into doing what she'd done, but that until offered the job by his former employer, he hadn't realized he'd been fooling himself about being ready to settle down in his old hometown. Both agreed things had ended for the best. And when his grinning brother later walked by, tucking his fists into his armpits, Cameron had popped him lightly on the back of the head and told him to knock it off.

Best of all, the Monday after the wedding, Lillian was offered the full-time librarian position. Cameron's Grandma Gray had capitulated to the recommendation of the other board members.

But it was now time to winterize the garden. To cut back the perennials that would lie dormant over the long winter ahead, knowing that again in the spring, they'd peep out of their protective mulch of leaves. The hyacinths usually first. Then the daffodils. Irises. Tiny leaves on the trees. As sad as it was for autumn's bright hues to fade away, ahead lay the promise of springtime.

A new start.

But with a heart every bit as barren as the garden would soon become, she couldn't imagine the dark days and cold, snowy months ahead without Denny's smile. His laughter. His encouragement. But he'd chosen to leave Hunter Ridge. To leave *her*.

"Lillian?"

She looked up to see Aunt Viola holding the back door open. Eyes twinkling, she looked like she'd explode with secret knowledge.

"There's *someone* here to see you."

Lillian's heart leaped.

Denny.

He came back.

Brushing at her wind-tangled hair, she looked down at her stained work clothes. Dirty sneakers. She was a mess.

But Denny is here.

Eagerly she got to her feet. "Where—?"

And then Taylor peeped out from behind her aunt.

Lillian gasped, her hand flying to her mouth and tears pricking her eyes. She stood frozen, disbelieving. And then she opened her arms and Taylor shot out the door, down the stone path and straight into them.

"Taylor, oh, Taylor." She held the girl close, reveling in the arms that clasped around her. That squeezed tight. "You're back. I can't believe it. You're really back."

"I'm never ever leaving again, Aunt Lillian." Taylor gave her another hug. "Mom said."

Still embracing the little girl, Lillian again looked to the back door of the inn. Aunt Viola had disappeared. But Annalise stood there on the steps, uncertainty filling her eyes.

Pulling away, Taylor grasped Lillian's hand and tugged her across the garden. "Tell her, Mommy, tell her!"

Annalise met them halfway, holding out her hand to her daughter. "Why don't you run in and help Aunt Viola fix our lunch?"

"But you'll tell her, won't you?" Taylor's eyes urged her impatiently.

Annalise smiled a little sadly. "Don't worry—I'll tell her."

Taylor hugged Lillian again, then her mother, before skipping to the back door and disappearing inside.

Lillian folded her arms, assessing her sister. "You're leaving her here again? After what we just went through?"

While Taylor's "never ever leaving" still echoed in her ears, she didn't dare let her hopes rise due to something that most likely was a misunderstanding on the part of a child.

"I want to leave her here, Lillian," Annalise said slowly. "That is, if you still think you want her."

Was her sister saying what she thought she was? "She's always welcome for as long as you're willing to share her." Lillian drew a breath as she unfolded her arms, then held out a hand in appeal. "I— Annalise, please believe me when I say I never would have taken her from you against your will. That was never my intention."

"You *should* have, Lil. A long time ago. I'm not cut out to be a parent. Never have been."

"You love Taylor. I've never doubted that."

Her sister shook her head. "Not the kind of love that has a child's best interests in mind. I'm sorry I acted ugly. Snatched her away from you. I don't know what got into me. I think it hit me hard when she was so excited about the possibility that she might get to stay permanently with you and that— What is his name?" Her brow wrinkled. *"Mister?"*

"Denny, actually." She couldn't help but smile. "He felt terrible that Taylor must have overheard us talking."

And witnessed that near-kiss.

"I admit when she told me about that conversation I was jealous. Extremely jealous."

"Why jealous? I can see why you'd be angry. You had every right to be."

"I was jealous because Taylor's heart is here. With you and Aunt Viola. And with a man she can't stop talking about. He must really be something, Lil. I'm jealous about that, too."

Now probably wasn't the time to confess he'd walked out on her. She'd let Taylor continue believing he was a hero for now, too. Who knew? Maybe he'd come back to visit her if Lillian could get word to him that her niece had returned.

"I guess I'm still confused, Annalise, about what this means."

"It means, with your permission, I'd like us to explore what needs to be done to give you full legal custody. To adopt her if you want to."

"Are you sure?" a stunned Lillian whispered.

"I've had enough time to think it through. I'd been thinking about it before I dropped her off with you in June. I've even *prayed* about it, sis. Isn't that a hoot?" She gazed at Lillian with love in her eyes. "You're good with her, Lil. And for her. You and Aunt Viola. Much better than I will ever be."

"But you're her mother. She loves you."

"And I love her. That's why I want to give her a chance at something I never had myself. The care and attention— and love—of a parent who will always be there for her."

"Mom and Dad did their best."

She gave a little snort. "You think so? Come on. Stop lying to yourself."

Had she been deceiving herself? Or with God's help, had she been able to extend forgiveness that Annalise didn't yet have the ability to offer?

"What if I fail? What if I turn out to be no more better of a parent to Taylor than they were to us?"

"I have no fear of that. But whatever you can give her will run circles around what the two of us got. What I'm capable of giving her. I promise I won't disappear out of Taylor's life and leave her feeling abandoned. But I'm not ready to settle down. Not for a long while." She made a silly face. "But who knows? Maybe eventually I'll get my act together."

And if she did? Would she be back to claim Taylor?

As if reading her mind, Annalise offered a reassuring smile. "I want you to have her. No strings attached. And I'll always let you know where I am and give you fair warning when I'm coming for a visit. If you advise me it's not a good time to come…well, that's your decision and I'll abide by it. Taylor might still call me Mom, but you're the mother her heart has chosen."

"I don't know what to say, Annalise. Except…" Her voice cracked as tears pooled in her eyes. "Thank you."

Annalise's eyes likewise filled as she held out her arms. "I need a hug from my big sister."

As Denny slipped through the back gate, Lillian drew back from a young woman he recognized as her sister, and he hoped the hug meant they'd made up. That Taylor had returned. Then, turning startled eyes in his direction, they stared as he stood gripping a large box easily in one hand.

"I'm sorry to intrude. I—"

"I thought you'd gone back to San Francisco," Lillian said softly, and his heart sang at the sound of her voice.

"Not yet." He'd spent the past three days hiking the mountain trails. Thinking. Praying. And last night had turned up on Pastor Garrett McCrae's doorstep. His cousin hadn't been the least bit surprised.

"This is Denny Hunter." Lillian motioned to him as he joined them. "Denny, this is my sister, Annalise."

Her sister wiped tears from her eyes with one hand and held out her other to shake his. "Good to meet you— *Mister.*"

The women looked at each other. Laughed. Wiped away the last of their tears.

"Time for lunch, girls!" Viola called from the back door. She waved to him. "You're welcome to join us, Denny."

She said the words as if she hadn't been surprised to see him there.

"I don't know about you two," Annalise said as she turned toward the inn, giving Lillian a thumbs-up and what he interpreted as a significant look, "but I'm starving."

To his relief, Lillian didn't follow her.

"Annalise is dropping Taylor off with you again? Didn't I say she would?" But he honestly hadn't expected for it to happen so quickly.

She nodded. "It's a long story you're not going to be—"

"I'm eager to hear it," he said, reaching for a surprised Lillian's hand and guiding her to a more secluded spot near the gazebo, "but not just yet."

Her eyes held a wary look, as if unsure what to make of his sudden appearance after the way he'd left her a few days ago. "What are you doing here?"

He placed the box on a nearby wrought-iron table. "Oh, you know, the usual stuff people do in an off-the-beaten-path little town. Going for walks. Gazing at the clouds. Counting the cracks in the sidewalk."

"Listening to crickets?"

"That, too."

"Seriously, Denny, why are you still here?"

"Unfinished business."

"Related to the inn?"

"You could say so. It took a little persuading, but once I gave her my word not to let Dad get his hands on it, my mother was good with selling the inn to me."

Her eyes widened. "*This* inn?"

"And the two buildings on either side of it." He had an eye on another property across the street, too, with a residence in mind. But he'd need to negotiate with the owner.

Her pretty mouth opened in surprise. "Why?"

He smiled. "Because a few days ago, a beautiful woman made me realize I've spent a lifetime protecting my little-boy heart. I've focused my energies on earning respect rather than accepting—and giving—love."

"I don't understand. What's that have to do with buying the—?"

"I've been hiking the forest trails for days—praying about what you said about my pushing people away. Being afraid to let others—and God—get close. Not just praying about it, but *really* praying about it."

"That's why you bought the inn?" She still sounded confused.

"It's why I had a long conversation with my cousin Garrett late last night. Realizing I was headed in a direction I didn't want to go and had to get on the right path, I made the decision to turn my life over to God." Denny's eyes were bright with hope. "I'll soon be joining a men's Bible study and will be baptized in Hunter Creek on Sunday, like I'm told my great-great-grandfather Harrison 'Duke' Hunter was. Like the other Hunters who have surrendered their hearts to their Maker. I decided I don't want to miss out any longer on what God wants to do with my life."

"You're taking your hands off the steering wheel and letting *Him* do the driving?"

"I am."

Her eyes smiled into his, and his heart rocketed. "Oh, Denny, I'm so happy for you."

"I woke up this morning feeling like a new man." He mimed a yawn and stretched his arms, as if awakening from a deep sleep. "Like a man who—someday, I hope—will be known as a man of faith, for his love of God and others. Not merely as a well-respected businessman."

"We see our faults," she whispered, "but He sees our possibilities. If we cooperate, He will change us into more than we could ever hope or dream."

"I have you to thank for helping me move in that direction, Lillian. You—and, unbelievably, my dad—opened my eyes to things I'd been blind to for way too long. Misconceptions. Erroneous beliefs. Things I understood in part. And among those things is the fact that God loves me whether I'm considered perfectly 'lovable' or not. Even when I'm at my most undeserving of love."

"None of us deserves love, Denny. It's a gift freely given."

"And *my* love is a gift I'm giving you, Lillian. That is, if you want it."

She stared at him, her eyes searching his, and he rushed on before he got cold feet. "Even though we've known each other a short time, I've come to love you more deeply than you will ever imagine. Do you think you could find it in your heart to forgive me for my stupid blunders? My shortcomings? The hurt I've dealt you?"

She swallowed, hesitated, no doubt getting snagged on the L-word. "Oh, Denny, of course I forgive you. And I need your forgiveness, as well. I'm not even close to being perfectly lovable, either."

His heart lightened as he plunged on. "And would you be willing to consider entering into a courtship that I pray will lead to spending the rest of our lives together—in Hunter Ridge?"

Doubt filled her eyes. "But you love the city. You thrive on its energy, the activity. The corporate chase."

"Overrated. And in fact…" Would she believe him when he told her? "I no longer want to play the game I've been playing for far too long. I quit my job this morning. Cut ties with GylesStyle Inns."

"You didn't."

He nodded. "I'm a free man, Lillian, in every way, shape and form."

"But what are you—? How are you—?"

"Going to earn a living? If you and your aunt are agreeable, I'd like to further expand the Pinewood Inn to the two adjoining buildings. Maybe open a bistro on the ground floor on one side. Then market it all to the max. The inn. The town."

"But I thought you said the Pinewood would never be profitable."

A smiled tugged at his mouth. "But as you may recall, I also said I've seen the most unlikely ventures succeed in the most improbable of locales, under good management."

"I remember."

"It will be a leap for sure, but Garrett tells me a life of faith is in many ways a life of taking risks. With my extensive innkeeping background and the assistance of a top-chef friend whose artist wife wants to get their kids out of the city, I'm cautiously optimistic. It won't be easy.

But if I give it all I've got and trust God to work beyond my limited abilities, I think we stand a good chance of making a go of it."

We. He liked the sound of that. *Please, Lord, let her buy into the dream.*

"If it can be done, Denny Hunter," she said without a hint of doubt, "you're the man who can do it."

"But I can't do it without you, Lillian. Nor do I want to try. Would you be willing to think it over? To pray—"

She shook her head, and his hopes dissolved. She wanted no part of the dream he'd laid before God. No part of *him.*

"I've done all the thinking—and praying—I need to." Her eyes now shining into his, she took a single step toward him. "I love you, Denny, with all my heart. And I want to spend the rest of my life loving you."

His heart soared, and without hesitation, he dropped to one knee.

"Will you marry me, Lillian?"

Tears pricked her love-filled eyes as she gazed down at him. "Oh, I will. I will."

Her words rang in his ears and filtered down into his heart, yet how tempting it was to ask her to repeat them again. To make sure he'd heard right.

Denny the unlovable, loved and accepted by the woman of his dreams.

"I love you, Lillian, and when I think of how close I came to losing you, I—"

"But we didn't lose each other."

He traced his finger down the third one on her left hand. "I'm afraid I don't have a ring for you yet. We'll get one. I promise. But I do have something else for you."

He stood to give her a lingering kiss, then drew her to the table where the box he'd brought with him rested.

She laughed. "That's a floor-tile box."

"That's all I had. But good things come in odd packages." He nodded to it. "Open it."

Raising the cardboard flaps, she then reached in for the tissue-paper-wrapped object that was clearly a book. She gave him a curious look.

"Go on."

Gently pulling back the yellowed paper, she stared down at the old black leather-bound volume in her hands. *Holy Bible*, the cover read in faded gilded lettering.

"It's the *treasure*, Lillian."

She shook her head, not understanding.

"The Newell family treasure. I found it in one of the walls we tore out. I was waiting for the right time to give it to you."

"This is what we've been searching for?"

"It is. Look here." He carefully opened the volume to the pages where births, marriages and deaths had been recorded. Then to the family tree. "Generations of your family, Lillian, from the late 1700s down to your great-great-grandparents."

"Oh, my," she whispered as she deciphered the faded ink. "This *is* a treasure."

"Generations of Newell descendants—evidence of lifetimes of long-lasting unions based on love and vows made before God."

"Aunt Vi will be thrilled."

"But I know she'll want you to have it—to pass down to the coming generations."

Their children. Grandchildren.

She closed the book, then reverently placed her hand

on its cover. "Why do you think Benjamin Newell hid this?"

"I don't know that he originally intended to hide it permanently. The place I found it was framed with a hinged door, and it looks as if it was engineered to be a place for keeping valuables and designed to blend in with the wallpaper."

"A wall safe of sorts?"

"Right. But somewhere over the years, that whole section of the wall was covered over with plywood, right over the top of the door and the wallpaper. No one probably knew it was there. That's pure speculation, of course."

"Why are you smiling like that?"

"Because I have another theory."

She gave him a mock threatening look, then laughed. "Don't hold out on me, *Mister*."

He laughed. "From studying the family tree, it appears this Bible was likely passed down through the generations to the oldest son bearing the name of Newell."

"Great-great-grandpa Benjamin Newell was an oldest son."

"And in looking at the births recorded, I saw that he had only daughters. No more Newell sons to carry on the name."

"So you think...?"

"He may have walled up the Bible himself rather than pass it down to a daughter who'd no longer bear the family name when she'd most likely marry."

She cringed. "Kind of sexist, huh?"

"Not necessarily. Perhaps a man to whom tradition was important. Or who didn't know which daughter to give it to."

She gazed down fondly at the old volume in her hands. "I guess we'll never know, will we?"

"What puzzles me, though, is that he'd apparently referred to a *treasure*. And let it be known it was hidden in the house."

Lillian nodded. "He mentioned it when he was dying several years after his wife passed away. That's what Aunt Vi says. He'd had a stroke. Could barely speak and didn't linger long."

"So he may have had a change of heart. Wanted one of his female descendants to have it after all." Denny took the book from her hands and placed it in the box on the table. "And now it's in your hands—his great-great-granddaughter. You've fulfilled his dying wish to pass it on to another generation."

He opened his arms to her, and without hesitation she stepped into his welcoming embrace. He held her for some moments, their hearts beating in unison. Then he briefly touched his lips to hers.

"I pledge my life and my love to you, Lillian, knowing that just like the many couples recorded in your Bible, God has a special plan for the two of us."

"The *two* of us," she murmured dreamily.

Then with a sudden gasp she pulled back, alarm lighting her eyes. "Oh, no. I almost forgot."

Apprehension shot through him. "Forgot what?"

"There's…there's something important you need to know about the future of the *two* of us."

But before she could continue, there came the sound of little-girl feet pounding down the walkway behind him.

And a giggle.

"Hey, Mister! *Denny!* I'm home—for good!"

Epilogue

"If you have your running shoes with you, it's not too late to make the great escape," a smiling Denny whispered as they stood in the Pinewood Inn's garden the evening before their June wedding day.

Softly illuminated by solar lights along the walkway and surrounded by the sweet scent of Aunt Viola's petunias, Lillian looked up into the eyes of the man she loved.

"Sorry, Mister, but I'm not letting you off the hook. I'm not going anywhere tomorrow afternoon—except down the church aisle and straight into your arms. *You'd* better be standing there waiting for me."

"I guarantee it. Lasso in hand."

With a laugh, she playfully poked him in the rib cage. "You think you're funny, don't you?"

Eyes twinkling, he took both her hands in his. "And I think *you're* beautiful inside and out. God truly blessed me when He brought you into my life. And I hit the jackpot with Taylor and your aunt thrown in."

He made her feel special. Treasured. "We're getting married tomorrow, Denny."

"That we are."

In less than twenty-four hours, vows taken and rings exchanged, they'd be dancing under the stars to a string quartet at a reception here in the garden of the Pinewood Inn.

What would life hold for them as they grew together in God? Church and community ministry. Building the recently expanded inn's reputation for hospitality. Sharing life with Aunt Viola. Raising Taylor.

Reba was thrilled when Lillian turned down the full-time librarian position, opting to stick with a half-time one. And Denny had been relieved when his bride-to-be didn't object to occasional trips to Phoenix for professional sporting events. He was more than happy to trade in his Porsche for a crew-cab pickup, too.

"I'm glad your mother and stepfather are coming tomorrow."

"Me, too, but we'll see how that goes over. Dad hasn't spoken to my mother except through an attorney for thirty years. And he's only met Elden once—twelve months ago, when God rescued me from making what would have been the biggest mistake of my life."

"But you said your folks are willing to call a truce, right?"

"So they say. I think the prospect of me settling down—and maybe producing a few grandkids—has them rethinking their priorities. Makes them more amenable to compromise."

Grandchildren. Denny's and her offspring. A tingle of anticipation raced through her.

But there would be adjustments on both their parts—two stubbornly independent people used to making their own decisions and calling the shots without consulting anyone else. Now, as in past months, they'd continue learning on a daily basis to take the other person into consideration, to unselfishly place the other's needs and welfare above their own.

A city boy and small-town-hearted girl.

"I hope the reality of giving up city life, your career, for Hunter Ridge doesn't disappoint you." She gently squeezed the strong hands that cradled hers. "That *I* don't disappoint you."

"Not a chance." He kissed her forehead. "Besides, I'll continue to do periodic contract work for GylesStyle and keep my toe in the hotel industry waters at large. Being forced to demote Vic last month has opened Elden's eyes to a lot of things."

"Including *your* value. He desperately wanted you to return for that vice presidency, didn't he? Pressured you hard." She stepped back to look him in the eye. "I don't know how you resisted."

"No significant resistance was required on my part. I am where I want to be. Doing what I want to do. Being with those I love and want to be with. I'm right where God wants me. And I'm proud as can be that my colleague Craig is stepping into that VP slot, and Barry is back on the job in Kansas City."

"You have to admit, though," she mused, "that life *is* a lot slower here."

"There are advantages to that, don't you think?" He tugged her closer, then slowly—very slowly—kissed her. Taking his time. Drawing out the sweeter-than-sweet moment. All too soon he drew back, his eyes smiling. "I think I can adjust to slow."

"I know I can," she said breathlessly as she pulled her hands free and slipped her arms around his neck to draw his mouth back down to hers.

But their lips had no more than touched when the light by the back door repeatedly flashed on and off, illuminating them like a strobe light.

"Break it up. Break it up."

"Garrett," they groaned simultaneously as they reluctantly pulled apart. Denny's cousin Grady had warned them that their pastor cousin would become a particular nuisance as their wedding day approached.

"There are small children on the premises." The voice came again.

"That's me," Taylor echoed with a giggle.

"You know, Preacher—" Denny squinted into the bright light where they could see a grinning Garrett standing in the doorway, his arm around Lillian's niece. "I still owe you a black eye. It wouldn't take much more provocation to deliver on it."

Garrett laughed. "Bring it on, coz. But keep in mind that your bride won't be thrilled if your officiating minister looks like a ruffian in the wedding photos."

Denny looked down at Lillian. "He has a point."

Lillian nodded. "A good one."

Shaking his head, Denny snagged her hand and drew it to his lips for a quick kiss. "Less than twenty-four hours."

"Nineteen hours and thirty minutes, to be exact. Then we'll have a lifetime together."

"I like the sound of that."

"Me, too."

Hand in hand, they headed back to the inn as a laughing Taylor raced out to meet them.

* * * * *

Find more great reads at www.LoveInspired.com

Dear Reader,

While Lillian may be the only one of the pair who chose to flee from the altar, both she and Denny clearly have "runaway hearts" needing to be healed. Despite a longing to love and be loved, both hold misconceptions about themselves and others that have built barriers only our loving Heavenly Father can break down. Only He can show them that they must first accept His love in order to unlock the bolted doors to their hearts.

Have *you* accepted the love God offers to you? He's there, ready and waiting, with open arms. For "this is love, not that we loved God, but that He loved us and sent His Son as an atoning sacrifice for our sins." There is no greater gift that's ever been given.

I must admit that saying goodbye to a beloved Arizona mountain town in this final book of the Hearts of Hunter Ridge series is bittersweet. It's been a time of change for the little community, and I've enjoyed exploring with you the lives and loves of the men and women who have always called this place home, who once fled its city limits and returned, or who stepped into the little community for the very first time—all with connections, either family or friend, to the Hunters of Hunter Ridge. I hope you've enjoyed your visits there, as well!

You can contact me at Love Inspired Books, 195 Broadway, 24th Floor, New York, NY 10007. And please stop by glynnakaye.com and Seekerville.blogspot.com, which is designated as one of *Writer's Digest* magazine's 101 Best Websites for Writers. We love readers, too!

Glynna Kaye

COMING NEXT MONTH FROM
Love Inspired®

Available April 17, 2018

THE WEDDING QUILT BRIDE
Brides of Lost Creek • by Marta Perry

Widowed single mom Rebecca Mast returns to her Amish community hoping to open a quilt shop. She accepts carpenter Daniel King's offer of assistance—but she isn't prepared for the bond he forms with her son. Will getting closer expose her secret—or reveal the love she has in her heart for her long-ago friend?

THE AMISH WIDOW'S NEW LOVE
by Liz Tolsma

To raise money for her infant son's surgery, young Amish widow Naomi Miller must work with Elam Yoder—the man she once hoped to wed before he ran off. Elam's back seeking forgiveness—and a second chance with the woman he could never forget.

THE RANCHER'S SECRET CHILD
Bluebonnet Springs • by Brenda Minton

Marcus Palermo's simple life gets complicated when he meets the son he never knew he had—and his beautiful guardian. Lissa Hart thought she'd only stick around long enough to aid Marcus in becoming a dad—but could her happily-ever-after lie with the little boy and the rugged rancher?

HER TEXAS COWBOY
by Jill Lynn

Still nursing a broken heart since Rachel Maddox left town—and him—years earlier, rancher next door Hunter McDermott figures he can at least be cordial during her brief return. But while they work together on the Independence Day float, he realizes it's impossible to follow through on his plan because he's never stopped picturing her as his wife.

HOMETOWN REUNION
by Lisa Carter

Returning home, widowed former Green Beret Jaxon Pruitt is trying to put down roots and reconnect with his son. Though he took over the kayak shop his childhood friend Darcy Parks had been saving for, she shows him how to bond with little Brody—and finds herself wishing to stay with them forever.

AN UNEXPECTED FAMILY
Maple Springs • by Jenna Mindel

Cam Zelinsky never imagined himself as a family man—especially after making some bad choices in his life. But in seeking redemption, he volunteers to help single mom Rose Dean save her diner—and soon sees she and her son are exactly who he needs for a happy future.

LOOK FOR THESE AND OTHER LOVE INSPIRED BOOKS WHEREVER BOOKS ARE SOLD, INCLUDING MOST BOOKSTORES, SUPERMARKETS, DISCOUNT STORES AND DRUGSTORES.

LICNM0418

Get 2 Free Books,
Plus 2 Free Gifts—
just for trying the Reader Service!

Love Inspired®

*Widowed single mom Rebecca Mast returns to her
Amish community hoping to open a quilt shop. She
accepts carpenter Daniel King's offer of assistance—but
she isn't prepared for the bond he forms with her son.
Will getting closer expose her secret—or reveal the love
she has in her heart for her long-ago friend?*

Read on for a sneak preview of
THE WEDDING QUILT BRIDE
by **Marta Perry**,
available May 2018 from Love Inspired!

"Do you want to make decisions about the rest of the house today, or just focus on the shop for now?"

"Just the shop today," Rebecca said quickly. "It's more important than getting moved in right away."

"If I know your *mamm* and *daad*, they'd be happy to have you stay with them in the *grossdaadi* house for always, ain't so?"

"That's what they say, but we shouldn't impose on them."

"Impose? Since when is it imposing to have you home again? Your folks have been so happy since they knew you were coming. You're not imposing," Daniel said.

Rebecca stiffened, seeming to put some distance between them. "It's better that I stand on my own feet. I'm not a girl any longer." She looked as if she might want to add that it wasn't his business.

No, it wasn't. And she certain sure wasn't the girl he remembered. Grief alone didn't seem enough to account for the changes in her. Had there been some other problem, something he didn't know about in her time away or in her marriage?

He'd best mind his tongue and keep his thoughts on business, he told himself. He was the last person to know anything about marriage, and that was the way he wanted it. Or if not wanted, he corrected honestly, at least the way it had to be.

"I guess we should get busy measuring for all these things, so I'll know what I'm buying when I go to the mill." Pulling out his steel measure, he focused on the boy. "Mind helping me by holding one end of this, Lige?"

The boy hesitated for a moment, studying him as if looking at the question from all angles. Then he nodded, taking a few steps toward Daniel, who couldn't help feeling a little spurt of triumph.

Daniel held out an end of the tape. "If you'll hold this end right here on the corner, I'll measure the whole wall. Then we can see how many racks we'll be able to put up."

Daniel measured, checking a second time before writing the figures down in his notebook. His gaze slid toward Lige again. It wondered him how the boy came to be so quiet and solemn. He certain sure wasn't like his *mammi* had been when she was young. Could be he was still having trouble adjusting to his *daadi*'s dying, he supposed.

Rebecca was home, but he sensed she had brought some troubles with her. As for him…well, he didn't have answers. He just had a lot of questions.

Don't miss
THE WEDDING QUILT BRIDE by Marta Perry,
available May 2018 wherever
Love Inspired® books and ebooks are sold.

www.LoveInspired.com

Looking for inspiration in tales
of hope, faith and heartfelt romance?

Check out **Love Inspired**® and
Love Inspired® **Suspense** books!

New books available every month!

LIGENRE2018